COALDALE PUBLIC LIBRARY

WITHDRAWN

Hooky and the Villainous Chauffeur

Hooky was relieved to find that the book bore singularly little relation to reality; who the hell wants art to echo life anyway, he thought? The business of art is to offer escape from reality; life made harsh enough noises itself without having to listen to echoes of the damned thing.

Thus Hooky Hefferman's philosophy, an outlook well suited to his role of amateur detective and professional adventurer.

Hooky arrives in the Sussex village of Sweeting by accident, the consequence of winning a bizarre bet and being nearly killed by a speeding limousine. Herbert Aston arrives there on purpose and in disguise, seeking revenge for a wrong done years ago to his dead brother, a wrong that had led indirectly to the suicide of Herbert's young niece.

The ruthless tycoon who had made himself squire of Sweeting village was soon seen to be the quarry they were both looking for. Others were looking for him too, and someone killed him.

It becomes Hooky's task to detect the murderer.

There had been adultery as well as murder in Sweeting. Hooky revels in the pastoral autumn climate of the village – the bar-room jokes, the cricket field now forlorn and abandoned for the winter – and also in the pursuit of a murderer.

The series of comedy-thrillers that have come lately from the experienced pen of Laurence Meynell have been a delight. Here is the same blend of humour, action and mystery, presented with splendid gusto.

by the same author

A VIEW FROM THE TERRACE (Hale)
THE FORTUNATE MISS EAST (Hale)
THE MAUVE FRONT DOOR (Collins)
THE DEATH OF A PHILANDERER (Collins)
OF MALICIOUS INTENT (Collins)
THE CURIOUS CRIME OF MISS JULIA BLOSSOM (Macmillan)
DEATH BY ARRANGEMENT (Macmillan)
A LITTLE MATTER OF ARSON (Macmillan)
THE FATAL FLAW (Macmillan)
THE THIRTEEN TRUMPETERS (Macmillan)
THE FAIRLY INNOCENT LITTLE MAN (Macmillan)
DON'T STOP FOR HOOKY HEFFERMAN (Macmillan)
HOOKY AND THE CROCK OF GOLD (Macmillan)
THE LOST HALF HOUR (Macmillan)
HOOKY GETS THE WOODEN SPOON (Macmillan)
PAPERSNAKE (Macmillan)

HOOKY AND THE VILLAINOUS CHAUFFEUR

A Hooky Hefferman Story

Laurence Meynell

M

© Laurence Meynell 1979

All rights reserved. No part of this publication may be reproduced or transmitted, in any form or by any means,without permission.

ISBN 0 333 25590 9

First published 1979 by
MACMILLAN LONDON LIMITED
4 Little Essex Street London WC2R 3LF
and Basingstoke
Associated companies in Delhi Dublin Hong Kong Johannesburg Lagos Melbourne New York Singapore and Tokyo

Printed in Great Britain by
The Anchor Press Ltd and bound by
Wm Brendon & Son Ltd
both of Tiptree, Essex

CONTENTS

CHAPTER ONE

Not exactly a love-nest

Sergeant Dillon took a last look at the dead girl's face and then pulled the grimy sheet over it. It wasn't the first time he had seen death and, since a subordinate was present, his rank demanded a show of indifference which he didn't actually feel.

P.C. Dale, a younger man, had not seen a corpse before and he was hovering between revulsion and fascinated curiosity.

'How old do you reckon she is, Sarge?' he asked.

'Twenty. Round-about. Could be a bit more, could be less. This game makes 'em look on the old side.'

'What do you reckon it is, then?'

'The usual formula, or some variation of it. Sure to be. Drugs and drink.' He indicated the chipped enamel mug that stood on an upturned wooden box by the side of the bed and the small glass bottle next to it. 'We'll have to find out what she was taking. Forensic will tell us. Vodka for a drink very likely. Might be meths. Could even be a mixture of the two. Vodka and meths! God Almighty, what those kids get up to nowadays.'

The Sergeant looked slowly round the room; it had once been a well-kept room in a well-kept house; but those days had long since passed. The square in which the house stood had come steadily down the social scale; from being once almost fashionable it had degenerated into being neglected and for the last four or five years had been little better than a slum.

When number twenty-nine became vacant (the tenant leaving without the formality of paying any rent) the agent entrusted with the business optimistically put up a 'For Sale' board. He didn't really expect to attract any custom by it but what it did attract was squatters.

And with the squatters came the inevitable hangers-on of squatterdom.

Any lingering relics of cleanliness or decency that might have persisted in the house were well and truly demolished by this last invasion.

The room round which Sergeant Dillon now looked had no furniture except the bed on which the dead girl lay and the wooden crate standing by it; three old sacks did duty as a carpet, the wallpaper was dirty and torn and served only as a blackboard for graffiti scrawled across it; the bedclothes consisted of a blanket and a sheet, both grimy in the extreme.

'Pretty sordid, isn't it?' Dillon said.

'Not exactly a love-nest,' the young constable agreed. 'Who's this chap the Badger, then, that we've got to see?'

The Sergeant gave a short, disillusioned laugh. 'He's a fly one is the Badger,' he answered. 'Properly educated. Not like you and me, underpaid ignoramuses. Knows it all. He knows more about the law and more ways of getting round the law than you and I have had hot dinners. He won't tell us anything, even if he could; but we've got to ask him all the same.'

'Head of this 'ere squatting lark, is he?'

'He'll deny it, but in effect that's what he is, yes.'

The Badger was waiting downstairs. He was tall and thin and he wore his hair shoulder length. He had a sensitive and intelligent face. He had been to a good school and, as the Sergeant had already said, 'knew it all'. He didn't like the law.

He listened to the opening questions and shook his head. 'No idea,' he said.

'You don't know who this girl is?'

'I've just told you – I've no idea.'

'You don't know her name?'

'She was called Frankie.'

'Frankie who?'

'I never bothered to ask – just Frankie.'

'Did you know her well?'

'Hardly at all. She lived her life, I lived mine; that's how I like it.'

'When did you last see her?'

'Three or four days ago, I forget exactly.'

'Was she an addict?'

'An addict? I don't know.'

'There's a hell of a lot you don't know, isn't there?'

'I don't know how accurately you use words, for one thing. At what precise point does anyone become an addict of anything? Frankie took drugs, yes; but how often?' He shook his head again. 'I don't know.'

'Did you see anything of her last night?'

'No, nothing.'

'Christ,' Sergeant Dillon said, 'you're a mine of information, you are. I suppose you can't get it into your head that the reason we are trying to find out something about this girl is to tidy things up and let her people, whoever they are, know what has happened; they're probably worrying themselves sick about her.'

'She must have come in some time yesterday evening.'

'How would she get in? Did she have a key, or would anybody let her in, or what? You don't know, of course, do you?'

'Yes, I do. She would come in through the basement door. It's always unlocked. Then I suppose she went upstairs to the bedroom and thought things over a bit and did what she did.'

'And you didn't see her until – what time this morning?'

'Haven't you people a record in the station of the time I rang up?'

'There'll be a note of that, of course.'

'Well, there's your answer; within five minutes.'

'Can you suggest any reason why she should have taken an overdose?'

'Plenty of reasons. Just go outside and take a good look round the whole bloody insane outfit.'

Sergeant Dillon snapped the elastic band over his notebook and put it away; for formality's sake he asked the essential question once again.

'And you've no idea of her full name or where she came from?'

'None.'

Outside, as they were getting into the police car, the young constable said, 'Not exactly matey, was he? What do we do next, Sarge?'

'Set the machinery in motion. There's quite a lot of machinery if you know how to make use of it. Mind you, the way these people live it's quite possible the Badger really doesn't know who the girl is, or where she comes from; but don't worry, we'll find it all out in time.'

They set the machinery in motion; a lot of visits were paid, a lot of questions asked, a lot of leg work done and in the end they found out what they wanted.

As far as the world in general was concerned the incident was of minimal importance and it was decently disposed of by a delayed entry in the *Deaths* column of the *Daily Telegraph*:

> *Frances Veronica Aston, aged 18. Only and beloved daughter of Maude and the late Edward James Aston of Pond Cottage, Little Newford . . .*

Although he was a lecturer in the University and could have had rooms in College, Herbert Aston preferred to live outside, in the town. He had what he called his 'digs' in a small house in Watchman's Row. A sitting room and a bedroom. Books so overflowed in the sitting room that there didn't seem to be anything else in it; the bedroom was spartan in its simplicity.

The Professor was looked after by Mrs Morris, a West Countrywoman, who was wont to say in her mothering fashion, 'Like a child, 'ee is; just like a child.' It was true in some ways; but if Herbert Aston did have some childlike traits and thought a whole lot of things not worth worrying about (what happened to his laundry, for instance, or what he was going to eat for tomorrow's dinner), he nevertheless possessed an extremely keen brain and a truly formidable will. His students made a certain amount of fun of him behind his back but even the most bovine of them was in no doubt at all about his ability to teach, or about his contempt for the modern world in which he found himself. 'He ought to have been a monk,' one of them once said, 'he'd have made a bloody good monk would our 'Erbert.'

In the roundabout way of the College grapevine the suggestion reached Aston himself and it amused him; indeed, he recognised a certain amount of truth in it, there were certain aspects of monastic life – discipline, hard living, dedication to an ideal – which appealed to him greatly.

It was Mrs Morris's duty to prepare the Professor's breakfast. This consisted, every day without variation, of cornflakes, one single rasher of Danish bacon, one and a half slices of wholemeal bread, Irish butter, honey and coffee. Early on, the good woman had tried to introduce some changes in the menu; she was reprimanded.

With the now completely standardised breakfast Aston read *The Times*, putting any post there happened to be on one side, unopened; in his opinion letters could always be dealt with later, and sometimes were. Letters could wait; but *The Times*' crossword demanded immediate attention; intellectual honour required that it should be solved before quitting the breakfast table.

But this morning there was no *Times*. The well-meaning newsagent had substituted a *Telegraph* and had scribbled on the top of the front page '*Sorry no Times*'. By such entirely fortuitous chances our lives are ruled – if a compositor working on the staff of *The Times* had not lost his temper; if the loss of temper had not escalated into a demand for an apology and subsequent 'industrial action'; if the local news-shop had not happened to have a spare copy of the *Telegraph* which could be substituted – *if*, exasperating and futile word; all these things did in fact happen, with the result that Herbert Aston found himself rather glumly studying an alien newssheet.

He turned to the crossword and saw at once that he wasn't going to enjoy it; there were no quotations and somehow the whole ambience of the thing was wrong.

Feeling rather like a child denied its customary toy, he abandoned the unsatisfactory crossword and let his eye wander unenthusiastically across the page. It fell by chance on the *Deaths* column, and suddenly to his astonishment his own surname stood out:

> *Frances Veronica Aston,* he read, . . . *the late Edward James Aston* . . .

aged eighteen, he reflected, what the devil do people mean by dying at eighteen? *Qui ante diem peruit* indeed; his niece, and he had never even seen the girl; and it was twenty-eight years since he had seen the late Edward James Aston, her father; this will hit Maude pretty hard, he thought. . . .

Aston himself was surprised at how much the chance piece of news had upset him, and he was profoundly relieved that the tutorial which he was due to take almost immediately was with Mrs Andrews.

Why Dorothea Andrews, aged forty, a widow and with a daughter, should be in the University reading for a degree in Eng. Lit. Aston didn't know; and, true to his settled creed of respecting other people's privacy as much as he wanted them to respect his own, he never enquired; he was more than content to accept the fact that this particular undergraduate as well as being highly intelligent had a sense of humour and was a mature person he could be friendly with.

He had asked her to write an appreciation of the technical excellence of Tennyson's poetry and she had submitted a clever and amusing essay.

'. . . better than I could have done myself,' he told her, winding up his commentary and criticism.

She laughed and made a deprecatory gesture with her hands, but she could not help being pleased.

'It's nice to be flattered,' she admitted.

Aston pulled a pipe out of his pocket, filled it and then laid it unlit on the arm of his chair.

'God knows what we are going to talk about today,' he said. 'I'm upset.' He hadn't meant to make this admission, and it was uncharacteristic of him to do it, so he added quickly, 'Not that I've any right to inflict my troubles on you. Do you read the *Telegraph*?' This also was something he hadn't meant to say but it had slipped out.

Dorothea, watching him with a woman's shrewd and compassionate eyes, nodded. Yes, she read the *Telegraph*. She had in fact noticed the name Aston in the *Deaths* column that morning. She said so.

'Ah well, my niece; but we needn't talk about it any more,' Aston said, reaching for his pipe.

'Why did she do it?'

'Do what?'

'Why did the girl commit suicide?'

The Professor laid his pipe down again still unlighted.

'*Suicide?* It didn't say anything about that.'

'But didn't you see the news item about it four or five days ago?'

Aston shook his head; there were days when the crossword was the only part of *The Times* he bothered about. The word *suicide* had upset him more than ever.

'What news item?' he asked.

'I noticed it because of the girl's name. My daughter's a Frances, too. This girl – your niece, was she? – was found dead in some sort of squatting commune; apparently she had taken a lot of drink and an overdose of sleeping tablets, barbiturates I suppose – but, of course, you must know all this.'

The man stared at her blankly without answering for some seconds, then, 'I know absolutely nothing whatever about it,' he was forced to confess.

'But she was your niece – ' Dorothea prompted gently and questioningly; even accusingly, he thought.

Aston didn't reply immediately; finally he said, 'Yes, she was my niece. And you may well be wondering about it all.

Looking back on it now it isn't a particularly edifying story; but then pride and mistaken ideas of honour usually land people in a mess, don't they? What else is most history?'

Dorothea Andrews was not interested in a general verdict on history, she was interested in the human being sitting opposite her, usually so much in command of himself, now clearly distressed and too agitated even to light his inevitable pipe.

'Tell me,' she suggested quietly.

'Edward, the girl's father, was five years older than me and I always looked up to him. I wasn't jealous in any way, I just thought he was the tops. *Sans peur et sans raproche.* I tended to be a romantic in those days, and romantics must have their heroes to worship. If anybody had come to me with a story about Edward doing anything dishonest I would have offered to fight them straight away; and, although I can see the necessity of it occasionally, by and large I'm not a person who likes fighting.

'The funny thing is I can't remember the first time I ever saw Maude. Probably it was at some teenage party. Tennis possibly. The sort of thing Edward was really good at and I just got by. But once she came on the scene she always seemed to be there.

'It suited me. I was seventeen, getting on for eighteen, and I fell in love with her.

'We were all three together an awful lot in those days – tennis, swimming, riding, all through the long summer months. I suppose I must have done some reading some time or I would never ultimately have got my degree, but looking back all I can remember is two years of sunshine and Maude.

'What astonished me was that she should prefer me to Edward; at least that was how it seemed to me; but then, as I say, I was a young man in love and young men in love are apt to get distorted ideas.'

'Yet it's not a bad complaint to suffer from – love,' Dorothea put in quietly.

'Is it not?' Herbert Aston said a trifle grimly. 'Well, maybe, maybe. But that's present wisdom; and, what is it? Twenty-eight years ago, I wasn't wise; I was young and in love. And almost unbearably happy because I thought I was loved in return. There's something in Shakespeare about love being blind – '

'Helena says it in *A Midsummer-Night's Dream.*'

'What I've forgotten about Eng. Lit. I can always come to you for. In *The Dream*, is it? That ridiculous play. Well, I was blind right enough. By this time I was twenty, and we had specifically come to an understanding, Maude and I, that we were going to marry. I must make that clear in self-defence of all I've done, or rather haven't done, since.

'It was to be kept secret, at any rate for the time being, because according to Maude her people would think we were both much too young. So nobody was to be told. I didn't mind that, in fact having a secret about it made the whole thing more exciting somehow.'

'Did your brother – did Edward know?'

'Oh, he knew all right – as subsequently became evident. I didn't specifically tell him because Maude had said *not a word to anybody, mind; not one single word to anybody*. I gave her my word of honour on it, so I couldn't tell anybody, not even Edward; in those days I had quaint ideas about honour. I've told you I was twenty, haven't I? Maude was the best part of a year older, just coming up to be twenty-one.

'Of course there were all sorts of preparations for her twenty-first birthday party. I suppose in comparison with the sort of thing young people are used to these days it would all look pretty simple. But everything was simpler then. God knows *I* was simple enough.

'The party was going to be on the actual birthday and after tea on the day before I cycled up to the Rectory – did I tell you her father was the local clergyman? A rural dean or some such creature. I wanted to leave my present for her before she got swamped with a whole lot from other people. The Rectory was a nice, old-fashioned place with a bit of a drive planted with rhododendron bushes and a croquet lawn where we all had lots of fun together.

'Maude wasn't there and Mrs Quayle, her mother, was surprised to see me.

' "I thought Maude was with you and Edward," she said.

'I shook my head; I hadn't seen Maude or Edward all afternoon.

' "Well, that's what she told me; she told me not to worry if she was a bit late, she was going to be with you and Edward." '

Herbert Aston picked up his pipe, lit it with rather more care than usual, and after puffing out the first cloud of soothing smoke went on, 'She was with Edward right enough because they ran off together, got married and settled down somewhere or other and I haven't set eyes on either of them since.'

Dorothea Andrews was entranced by this totally unexpected glimpse of the Professor's private life. Entranced and disturbed by it; even shocked.

'How long ago was all this?' she asked.

'Twenty-eight years.'

'And in twenty-eight years you have never made up the quarrel?'

'Maude did write one letter to me shortly after it all happened. Explaining – that's what she called it – why she had to act as she had done. I never answered it. I tore it up. How do you "explain" an act of treachery like that?'

Dorothea stared at the short compact figure hunched in the familiar posture in the chair. Short, compact and, she realised for the first time, powerful. She reflected on the amazing unpredictability of human beings; this man whom hitherto she had regarded simply as a fount of amusing and thought-providing opinions on Eng. Lit. turned out to be as capable of passion, hatred and determination as anyone else.

'Twenty-eight years,' she repeated, 'and you've had nothing to do with one another in all that time?'

'Nothing. When Edward died I saw the notice in the paper but I didn't go to the funeral.'

'And you were his brother.'

'And loved him once.'

Dorothea made no comment on that statement; after a pause she asked, 'And this girl, your niece don't forget, who took her own life, what about her?'

'I've never even seen the girl.'

'How do you suppose her mother is feeling?'

Herbert Aston made no reply.

His pupil began to gather her papers and books together. She stood up and faced him. His pupil no longer. A mature woman with the wisdom and compassion which belong to a woman.

'I think that's a pretty dreadful story,' she said. 'I can't be bothered any more today about how clever Tennyson was at managing internal vowel sounds. There are more important things than being clever. You know what you must do, Professor, don't you? In all decency and humanity you must go and see this girl's mother. You must go and see her and tell her the past is all finished and forgotten, except the good things in it, and you must see what you can do to comfort and help her.'

She was astonished when she opened the front door and saw him. She recognised him at once as he did her – *Although she's aged*, he thought with a twinge of conscience, *life's knocked her about a bit* . . .

Two long seconds passed in silence, then 'Bertie,' she cried, and burst into tears.

It was a small house, ill-furnished. When they were sitting together in the little living room even the Professor, who usually didn't pay attention to these things, couldn't help noticing the shabbiness of the furniture.

Twenty-eight years had rolled away and miraculously they were back where they used to be. Or nearly. But of course it was different; they slipped easily enough into intimacy, but now there was no passion.

They talked about the eighteen-year-old girl who had recently provided work for the local coroner.

'. . . she never knew her father; she was born two months after he died. Otherwise it might have been so different, but there you are – I don't know; what happens to the young these days, Bertie? She and I never seemed to have any fun or happiness together at all. Just frightful scenes. Nothing simple. Croquet – remember how we used to enjoy that? Heavens, mention *croquet* to the lot poor Frances got caught up with and can't you hear them sneering and laughing. If only Edward had lived – '

'I ought to have come to his funeral.'

'I hoped you might; but I didn't think you would. Not after the way I had treated you, Bertie. Things done can't be undone. I realise that. It's no use saying *I'm sorry, forgive me*, nevertheless I do say it.'

Herbert Aston nodded; there was a good deal of forgiveness wanted on both sides, he thought.

'Tell me about Edward,' he said.

'Edward was a wonderful person.'

'When we were all young together, in those two golden summers,' Herbert said, 'I thought he was a god. If Edward had been Raffles I'd have been his Bunny gladly.'

The woman laughed a little harshly. 'It's been a long time since I had any golden summers,' she said. 'I've forgotten what they looked like. Edward died of T.B. I didn't think people had T.B. these days; but they do; Edward did, and he died of it. If we had had money it would all have been different; and we ought to have had money and a great deal of it.'

'Edward was always the practical one. I felt sure he would make a fortune,' his brother said.

'He did – for other people. You remember how mad he was about gadgets of any kind? Making and mending things. Especially anything electrical – '

Herbert Aston nodded.

' – I never knew what it was he was trying to invent at the moment,' Maude went on, 'because I don't understand the first thing about machines or electricity. And in any case what I was concerned about was Edward's health. We hadn't been married much more than a year before the first signs of the thing began to show. I didn't believe it at first. I didn't believe Edward could be *ill*. Neither did he. We were young and we laughed at the idea. Are you a religious person, Bertie?'

'Not in the slightest.'

'I am. I turned to religion after Edward died. I believe in sin and retribution for sin. I believe that all that has happened to me – including this latest horrible affair – is a retribution for what I did to you twenty-eight years ago – '

'Maude, for God's sake!'

'There you are, you see. In one breath you are telling me that you are not in the least religious, in the next you are calling on God.'

'Let's leave God out of it, shall we, and stick to what happened to my brother.'

'We had very little money, and nobody was helping us. My parents were shocked at what I had done – and why shouldn't they be with my twenty-first birthday party all arranged and paid for and I wasn't there? – and, of course, your people hated me for it, too. Edward and I didn't care. We had one another and he was going to make lots and lots of money. He was so busy and working so hard that we couldn't afford to pay attention to signs of illness. Being ill would get in the way of what Edward was doing, and he was much too excited about his work to allow that.

'If you look out of the window – only please don't because the garden is a jungle, I never do a thing to it, I haven't had the heart – but if you *did* look you'd see a shed against the wall at the end. It was Edward's workshop. That's where it began. He was in there all hours. Half the night often enough. Sometimes he had somebody to help him, a fanatic like himself, but mostly he was on his own. Do you watch TV?'

'Television?' The question took the Professor by surprise; he shook his head. 'No, it seems to me to be such an unnecessary amplification of mediocrity.'

'Good old Bertie! The same as ever. But people do watch it, you know. Lots and lots of them. That's why Edward concentrated on it; he said, "There's one in practically every home, so if I can think up something which every TV set needs I'm bound to be on a winner." And in the end he did think it up.

'I'm not going to say he invented it because Edward himself didn't like the word *invention*. He said "invention" always made him think of the man who jumped out of his bath and ran about naked, shouting out that he had discovered something. And Edward said it just didn't happen like that. Suddenly. You worked away at a problem for months and months, years maybe, and all the time you were getting a little nearer – if you were lucky – to the thing you wanted. You knew what you wanted, he used to say, and very often you knew the steps you would have to use to get them, it was just a question of getting the steps in the right order.

'Well, in the end he did it.

'Don't ask me to explain *how* the thing works. I haven't the faintest idea, any more than I have about how the telephone works. It's an electrical device, some modification built into a TV set which makes everything stand out three dimensionally. It makes TV into a 3D affair and it's as much an advance on the old flat screen as colour was on black and white.'

'Is it this thing called Threedy one sees advertised so much?' Aston asked.

'The man who stole it called it that. In the beginning Edward called it Notas, an anagram of Aston. Once he had got it to work properly he thought our fortune was made. So did I. I imagined people would be queuing up outside the shed in the garden to buy the idea. In actual fact not one single person came to look at it. Poor Edward very soon found out that inventing something is only just the beginning. The real hard, punishing fight comes afterwards – in trying to market the thing.

'Edward went slogging round to any number of firms, the big people first and then some smaller ones.

'By this time he was ill and getting steadily worse and he used to come home dead beat. It got to the stage when I dreaded hearing his key in the door and having to look at his face when he came in. Very often he had not even been given the chance to explain the thing, let alone show how it worked. "Cranks come in here pretty well every week with some crack-pot idea or other," they told him. "If we spent our time listening to them we would never get any work done."

' "Could I see the production manager?" he would ask; but the production manager was always in conference, or not back yet from an executive luncheon, or on the phone.

' "But isn't there anybody here interested in a new idea?"

'That always made them laugh. "It's all we can do to keep up with the old ideas," they assured him, "without bothering about anything new."

'One or two firms did have at least half a look at the idea; but they couldn't be persuaded to put any money into it – "Think what it's going to cost," they said, "and in any case you'll be up against the big boys, they'll never let you put this thing on the market, it would knock their sales to hell."

'By the end of that first winter I wished Edward had never had his bright idea; he had to go into the chest hospital for a time and I was terrified. But as soon as he came out again things took a turn for the better. A small firm in one of the new industrial estates in Sussex became interested and it really looked as though we had got started at last.

'Edward was a different person for a while; even his health got better. He had thought up one or two improvements on his original idea and he was busy working away at those whilst the man in Sussex attended to all the legal side of it and the paper work and he signed what they told him to sign.

'After a time he did begin to worry a little; after the first excitement of getting somebody interested things were dragging again. They told him not to fuss, all these things took time and everything would be all right in the end and so on.

'Then he had to go into the chest hospital again, and this time it was worse and he was in longer than before. When he came out everything was disastrous. The Sussex firm had got into trouble; they had an enormous overdraft and the bank was pressing for repayment. And there was some business of a big overseas contract they had been expecting to land, and had counted on, that never materialised. I never knew all the details; nor did Edward; well, for one thing, he wasn't told, then he was simply told that the firm had been taken over by one of the big companies and that the man who used to run it had been bought out and had gone.

'The news absolutely floored him of course, and all but sent him back into hospital.

' "What about my idea?" he asked. "What about Notas?"

'Believe it or not, at first he couldn't find out anything about Notas. There didn't seem to be anybody around who had ever heard of it. It took him a long time to discover what had really happened to the Sussex firm. We got lawyer's letters about mergers and take-overs and holding companies – things which meant absolutely nothing to me and precious little to Edward.

'You can guess what this was doing to anyone in Edward's condition. I saw him dying day by day in front of my eyes. The worst part was the frustrating sense of helplessness. There were all these long lawyers' letters and the printed documents which didn't really tell you anything. You couldn't make out who was who, or what the true position was.

'At last – this was months later and poor Edward was back in hospital again, worse than ever – something did begin to be clear; there was this huge concern called Videx; they seemed to own every sort of thing and they had bought up the little Sussex firm almost as an afterthought. Just the sort of outfit which Edward disliked and mistrusted anyway. He insisted on getting up out of hospital, which all the doctors told him was madness, and going to see them. They tried to put him off, of course, but he was so ill he was desperate. By this time he had almost given up hope of getting any actual money; he wanted to see some sort of justice done and to get some satisfaction.

'In the end he fought his way through and managed to see the man at the head of it all, somebody called Matton. He turned out to be just the sort of man Edward hated and despised, what he used to call a *tycoon*.

'Of course Edward never stood a chance. He knew nothing about big business and he was honest. First of all this man Matton denied that such a thing as Notas existed and maintained that he had never heard of it. Then he said that in any case this huge company of his, Videx, had bought up the Sussex concern lock, stock and barrel, so anything and everything the Sussex firm owned had automatically become his and had been paid for.

'Edward tried to point out that he himself had never agreed to the sale of his idea to anybody, he hadn't properly understood all the legal things that were going on and had signed whatever documents he was asked to sign.

' "More fool you," Matton said and just laughed at him. He was a dying man, of course, and they could see that he was dying, so why should they bother?'

Maude stopped speaking and a long silence ensued. Then Herbert said, 'I ought to have come to the funeral.'

'Ah, *"ought"*. A pretty futile sort of word, isn't it? Long ago I ought not to have treated you the way I did, so maybe things even out. I've come to think that on the whole things *do* even out in life, people tend to get what they deserve.'

'Edward didn't.'

'No, Edward didn't.'

'And this man Matton, did you get in touch with him after Edward died?'

'I tried to. I wrote to the firm. All I got back was a solicitor's letter saying that the whole affair had been dealt with already and that everything belonging to the Sussex firm was now the legal property of Videx.'

'And you've never had any money from Videx, from Matton?'

'Not a penny; and I never shall have now.'

'Probably not,' the Professor said, and after a pause he added, 'But you never know. I don't like high-powered tycoons any more than Edward did.'

CHAPTER TWO

Approaching a village

VIDEX – the name stood out across the front of the London office in aggressive gilt letters. Deliberately over-large letters, chosen personally by the head – and founder – of the firm, who liked things to be brash and assertive.

Just the one word. In the inevitable tangle of deeds and documents phrases such as *limited stock company*; *corporation* and the like necessarily appeared; the law demanded them, and although Frederick Matton had very little respect for the law when it got in his way he was shrewd enough to be careful to keep on the right side of it when necessary.

But on the outside of Videx House just the single word for the world to gape at and envy.

Envy which Matton didn't in the least resent, in fact he welcomed it. He understood envy. Envy was the natural tribute from someone who hadn't got on to someone who had. Envy, malicious gossip, even hatred; if you got to the top you attracted those – what of it? The big, burly, hard-living man shrugged them off. If he thought about them at all they amused him; they were the feelings he himself was perfectly capable of harbouring against anyone who crossed his path.

It was mid-afternoon on a September day and outside even the grimy old city took on a certain mellowness from the kindly sunshine.

Donaldson, the chief accountant of Videx, had been closeted with his chief for a gruelling half-hour. He had already realised that the advice he ought to give was not going to prove acceptable, so he saved his breath by not giving it, or at any rate by not trying to insist on it; but as a final shot he did venture to say,

'The board won't like it, Sir Frederick.'

COALDALE PUBLIC LIBRARY

'Sod the board.'

Donaldson nodded. It was the answer he expected; not of much practical value, but entirely in character.

'I haven't got where I am by being afraid of boards of directors,' Matton elaborated. 'I'll fix the board.'

The chief accountant nodded again; if past history was anything to go by, he thought it extremely likely that the chairman *would* fix the board. Something about the way the man nodded annoyed Matton, and he didn't propose to let the interview end without getting in an unpleasant dig. He didn't like Donaldson and he reflected with grim satisfaction that the man as yet had no idea of the nasty jolt that was coming his way.

'Incidentally,' Matton said, 'what time did that assistant of yours get 'ere this morning?' He still occasionally dropped an aitch, especially when he was cracking the whip.

'A bit late, I'm afraid,' Donaldson answered. 'I understand he's having some trouble at home.'

Matton shook his head violently. 'I'm not interested in people's troubles at home,' he said. 'I don't interfere in their private lives and I don't want their private lives interfering with the work they ought to be doing here for me at Videx. Come on time or don't come at all. Tell 'im, will you?'

This time the accountant didn't nod; in a dead, flat voice he said simply, 'I'll tell him, Sir Frederick.'

'What time are you flying to Paris tomorrow?' Matton asked.

'Round about half past four or five. I haven't had flight confirmation from Gatwick yet. I want to have the morning at home to get all the papers together; then I'll come up here directly after lunch to look at my letters and I'll be leaving for the airport in time to catch the plane.'

Matton nodded; he turned some matters over in his mind, suppressed a smile which he felt inclined to indulge in, and said:

'I'll send Tranter to pick you up at two.'

'No need to. I can manage in my own car O.K.'

'Never refuse a good offer, Donaldson. Use my Mercedes and save yourself some running expenses.'

'That's very good of you, sir.'

This time Matton allowed himself to smile.

When his accountant had left the room Matton glanced at the digital clock on his desk and watched it flick up four twenty-one.

There were plenty of days when half past six or seven found him still in his office, but this wasn't to be one of them. He pressed the lever of the intercom and spoke to his secretary.

'I'm going to the club for a rubber of bridge and then home. Unless there's a god-damned earthquake I don't want to be bothered. I'll be staying in the country tomorrow.'

'Very good, Sir Frederick.'

'I'll take a cab to the club. When Tranter comes with the car tell him to call for me there at six-thirty.'

'Very good, Sir Frederick.'

At the club in St James's, Scot, the hall porter, said in his quiet voice, 'Good afternoon, Sir Frederick.'

Matton only grunted; he didn't like the tall, dignified hall porter; 'supercilious bastard' was his mental verdict on him; he found it infuriating that the man refused to be impressed. 'If you want to see a real dyed-in-the-wool, god-damned snob,' he was wont to say, 'you can't beat one of these ever so bloody correct, old-fashioned servants, the sort who pride themselves on knowing their place and enjoy grovelling in it.'

'Anybody in the card room?

'Some of the members went up there after lunch, Sir Frederick.'

'When my man calls for me I'll be up there.'

'I'll see you are told as soon as the car comes, Sir Frederick.'

Scot was left alone again with his task in hand (sorting through the unclaimed and out-of-date mail) and his thoughts. He knew a good deal about Frederick Matton, as indeed he did about most members of the club: there was the start at fifteen as a barrow boy in the Edgeware Road; three years later the ex-barrow boy had set up in antiques and was making money; he was already showing himself to be one of those people who mysteriously attracts money and have the knack of generating it. By the time he was twenty-one Matton had made his first venture into the property market and had announced his intention of becoming a millionaire. Four years later he was well on his way there and was already known as a whiz-kid causing ripples in the City. Matton understood the City and enjoyed it. You took risks; you made your own decisions; you stuck to them; it was a fight and if you fought hard enough and kept on fighting you won through. Jungle warfare. For the people who didn't win through it was just too bad; in Frederick Matton's philosophy losers lost and that's all there was to it; he didn't have any time for losers.

Before he was thirty he was in the big time financially. A whole series of trusts, transfers, holding companies and take-over bids had put him close to his million. The empire he had created was bewildering in the inter-complexities of its finance; if some parts of it began to show signs of having shaky foundations they were got rid of, generally at a profit, and if subsequently they ended up disastrously Matton was grimly amused. 'Only a sucker would have bought that,' he would say, 'and suckers deserve to go bust, it's what they are there for.'

Ultimately the Matton empire became consolidated into Videx; the name went up in three-foot gilt letters to announce success to all and sundry in the City streets and the name of Frederick Matton went into the Prime Minister's Honours List; something of what he had done to earn his title could be read in his *Who's Who* entry – not everything, perhaps, but enough to give an air of respectability to the thing.

In the card room three men were waiting for a fourth to make up the table and Matton was welcomed.

The cut was made for partners and the deal was begun.

'What are we playing for?' Matton asked. 'A quid?'

The small, precise man opposite him, with a neat imperial beard, replied at once. 'The club stakes are twenty pence,

Matton; and I have no intention of breaching club rules.'

Matton nodded; blasted little lecturer or schoolmaster of some sort, he thought, probably not earning more than four or five thousand a year; less than chicken feed; if ever I thought it worth while to get on the committee of this outfit I'd shake the place up a bit; and I hate men with those little pokey beards anyway; twenty pence! Christ, that's what's wrong with this country, we're twenty-pence minded . . .

Nevertheless, he enjoyed his game of bridge, not least because when the arrival of his car was announced by Scot over the wall telephone he was winning comfortably. When the card-room door closed on his exit one of his opponents said in tones of exasperated envy, 'That chap must be the luckiest card holder in London,' whereupon the man with the neat imperial beard added his dry comment – 'The devil looks after his own, they say.'

Matton's car was roomy, comfortable and powerful; as he climbed into the back of it he uttered one word only – not 'home' which most men would have used, but simply the name of the house where he lived – 'Leys.'

Roger Tranter, the man in the driving seat, neither required, nor expected, any further instructions or conversation. His job was to drive the big car into the country as fast as possible, a thing he enjoyed doing, for he was an expert driver and just as much a devotee of speed for the sake of speed as was the man who employed him.

Tranter had once spent three months in Wandsworth Gaol for assault, a fact which did not worry Frederick Manton in the least; in his opinion the world could do with a bit more assault in it all round.

He sat smoking and studying the *Financial Times*, a paper which frequently made him violently angry but for which, nevertheless, he had a grudging respect. He paid no attention whatever to the hideous sprawl of outer London that slid by the car windows – the synthetic, plastic, characterless High Streets appearing one after another. There were long rows of box-like little houses where people lived on the side of the traffic torrent; occasional pedestrian bridges to get across from one side to the other; every now and again traffic lights which made Tranter swear under his breath if they were against him.

At last tattered remnants of nature began to appear – a few bits of neglected grass, a badly cut hedge or two and then some forlorn fields.

When they had been travelling for rather more than an hour they were in the blessed darkness of real countryside; now Tranter's head-lamps showed dim masses of trees and tall hedges lining the narrow lanes. It had rained heavily during the day and the roadway was still wet with puddles of water lying everywhere.

They were now approaching the village of Sweeting where Matton lived in a large and extravagantly equipped house known as Leys.

As usual, Tranter was driving the Mercedes faster than he should have done, and certainly much too fast for the narrow, twisting lanes that surrounded Sweeting; and, as usual, the man in the back of the car reading the *Financial Times* was not taking the slightest notice of the roads along which he was being driven. As far as Frederick Matton was concerned a road was simply an inconvenience between the London office and Leys, a nuisance to be got over as soon as possible. A startled '*Jesus*' was jerked out of him as the Mercedes suddenly swerved violently and an ominous scraping noise of briar hedge against polished paintwork came from the off-side.

'What the hell are you doing?' Matton demanded.

'One of those bloody hikers,' the chauffeur growled. 'Didn't see him till I was right on him round the bend of the lane.'

'We didn't hit him, did we?'

'Damn nearly. All but. Serve the silly so-and-so right if we had done. What the hell do they want to go walking round these narrow lanes for? He got a pretty good splashing out of the puddle, anyway.'

'Who was he?'

Tranter felt very much like answering '*How the hell am I supposed to know who the silly bugger was?*' but he let the question go unanswered and contented himself with grumbling, 'And what about my paintwork? Didn't you hear the hedge scraping against us?' Matton wasn't interested in the paintwork; it was the chauffeur's job to look after that; that was one of the things he was paid for.

A light was showing in the Lodge as they turned into the drive entrance; the big ornamental gates which had once stood there had been done away with long since and a cattle grid rattled under the heavy car as it sped through.

When they drew up outside the house Matton gathered together his *Financial Times*, his brief-case and a company report he had been studying.

'Any orders for tomorrow?' the chauffeur asked.

'I shan't be going to London tomorrow. But I want you to look after Mr Donaldson. He can't use his own car for some reason so you must pick him up at his house just after lunch, not a minute later than two, then run him up to the office and wait till he's ready to go to Gatwick. He's flying round about four, or four-thirty. He'll tell you the exact time tomorrow.'

'And what about you?'

'I'm going to have a day down here looking into the home farm; if I'm not careful I shall be ruined the way it's being run.'

A bleak smile played for a moment over Roger Tranter's face; somehow he didn't think his employer was in any danger of being ruined.

'Which car shall I take?' he asked.

'You had better take the Mercedes,' Matton told him, 'you enjoy driving that.'

It was in the nature of a sop to Cerberus; having the Mercedes to drive for half the day would put the chauffeur in a good temper, and although Frederick Matton didn't normally worry much about what sort of temper other people might be in he had his reasons for keeping Roger Tranter in a good mood.

The last five miles had been tough; the last two sheer hell.

It had all looked so different in El Vino's. Not that Hooky frequented El Vino's much these days; he had transferred his midday devotions to the Magpie in Mercer's Court, where Rosie, a dark, slim nymph with lustrous eyes, listened in flattering fascination to Hooky Hefferman's account of Hooky Hefferman's quixotic brushes with life; but occasionally he paid a visit to the old sounding board to see if the same old boasts were being made, the same old lies being told.

At first glance he thought there was nobody there that he knew; which gave him a jolt. Who the hell are all these youngsters, he thought, and then relief came as he caught sight of Lewis.

Lewis weighed sixteen stones, needed two stools to sit comfortably at any bar (he seldom sat anywhere else) and had once given it as his opinion that (next to any form of political speech-making) fresh air was the most noxious influence a man could expose himself to. Lewis in his day had been the editor of two literary magazines, both of which had failed, and it was his boast that he could write better parodies drunk (which he frequently was) than anybody else sober.

People occasionally speculated about his age but without coming to any satisfactory conclusion; usually they contented themselves by saying that he was a left-over from an older generation, a view which gained support from the huge black Homburg hat and the actor-manager type of cloak which he wore with untidy bravado.

'Amigo,' he greeted Hooky in salutation. 'It's a relief to see a serious drinker among these chattering children.'

Lewis himself was drinking wine. A bottle of claret stood before him. No one had ever known him drink anything other than wine and no one had known anybody drink more of it. He explained his attitude in the matter (as he explained many things in life) by a quotation:

> Feast on wine or fast on water
> and your honour shall stand sure
> God Almighty's son and daughter
> he the valiant, she the pure;

if an angel out of Heaven
  bring you other things to drink,
thank him for his kind attention,
  go and pour them down the sink.

'Doggerel, of course,' Lewis would say (and indeed said again now, for he repeated the lines to Hooky), 'but who writes doggerel of that quality nowadays? Come to that, who has heard of G.K.C. nowadays? G.K.C. would have eaten this lot in here before breakfast and not known he had anything – who's that little homunculus gabbling so fast at the end there?'

Hooky knew who the little man was because he recognised his voice.

'Don't you listen to the radio at half past seven every morning?' he asked.

'God forbid. *Half past seven!* My dear Hooky, at that hour I am only just reconciling myself to the fact that I am still alive and that there is another day to get through. Don't tell me that people are actually broadcasting then!'

Hooky laughed; Lewis was a character and characters must be allowed their little games of pretence.

'You ought to listen to what he's saying,' he urged. 'Do you good; he's a keep-fit merchant.'

A few paces away Selwyn Klein was in full spate; he had recently persuaded Broadcasting House to give him a spot in the early-morning programme and his four-minute pep talk every day on how to keep fit had caught the public fancy. He was talking in the fast, excited manner of a man very well pleased with himself and with what he was saying.

'The Gospel according to St Muscle,' Lewis said sardonically. He was beginning to take an interest in what was being said and Hooky, in spite of his recommendation on the subject, didn't altogether welcome the fact. It all depended on how much liquor the old toper had absorbed; if the claret-level inside him was too high he was apt to get quarrelsome and even aggressive.

'. . . and the finest exercise of all, the very best possible way of getting and keeping fit is something which nobody does these days – walking.'

'Balls.'

The interruption startled Klein who found himself confronted by the heavily built man who had moved down from the far end of the bar.

'Is this the sort of stuff you disturb honest citizens' sleep with at whatever ghastly hour it is every morning?' Lewis demanded. 'You ought to be prosecuted under the Trades Description Act. The only sensible way to stay healthy is never to walk a yard if you can avoid it and to drink at least one bottle – preferably two – of good claret every day; and as for saying that nobody walks these days – rubbish!'

Klein was beginning to assemble his forces after the first shock of attack. He looked round him; people were prepared to be mildly interested in what looked like being an amusing confrontation.

'I'll just lay you ten to one that nobody in this bar is prepared to walk twenty miles a day for seven consecutive days,' he said.

'I'll take that,' Lewis answered promptly. 'In fivers.'

Hooky was faintly disturbed. The old lunatic, he thought, what's he letting himself in for now? Twenty miles a day? Five miles in a day will finish him off for good if he's fool enough to try it.

Selwyn Klein thought so, too. 'So when do you start?' he enquired. 'I'll keep them posted on the radio every morning of how you are getting on. Don't forget to notify the first-aid people, they'll want to know where to send the ambulance.'

Lewis stared at him in marvellously simulated astonishment.

'My dear young wireless prattler,' he said in the tones of a headmaster reprimanding a presumptuous member of the Upper Fourth, 'you don't really suppose that I am intending to take part in this idiocy, do you? I haven't the time; I'm far too busy drinking myself to death and preparing my soul for whatever is going to happen when I have achieved that feat.'

'I understood you to take the bet.'

'Of course I took your silly bet and I shall be very pleased to relieve you of fifty pounds in due course. My friend here, who in spite of years of dissipation still remains distressingly muscular, will be delighted to walk twenty miles a day for seven consecutives days and so win fifty pounds for me, won't you, Hooky?'

Hooky Hefferman was so constituted that this was precisely the sort of idiotic challenge which he was incapable of refusing. He didn't bat an eyelid as he answered stoutly, 'Of course.'

Later, in private session with Lewis, he remonstrated, but more in resigned amusement than in real protest.

'What the hell have you let me in for now?' he demanded.

Lewis carefully filled two glasses from a fresh bottle of claret.

'It was necessary, absolutely necessary, to take that broadcasting little twerp down a peg or two,' he said. 'I'm sure you see that; necessary for the honour of honest rogues and bastards.'

Hooky grinned and raised his glass. 'Nothing like drinking your own health,' he said. 'Here's to honest rogues and bastards – but think of my poor feet!'

He had been thinking of his poor feet for some time past now. They had served him faithfully for six days, indeed for nearly seven days, because as closely as he could estimate he was in the one hundred and fifty-seventh mile of the lunatic task which Lewis had let him in for in El Vino's. When he reached the village of Sweeting, which he was slowly and painfully approaching, the task would be completed, and, according to Lewis, the honour of rogues and bastards vindicated.

The astonishing thing was, looking back on it all, that he had actually enjoyed it. Or most of it. There had been bad moments, of course; but to his surprise Hooky had discovered that to go on foot through the best part of a hundred and fifty miles of English lanes and byways had proved to be one of the most rewarding experiences of a life by no means lacking in incident.

This last day, the seventh, had been the worst. It had rained heavily most of the day, and since noon a blister had developed on his right heel so that walking had become excruciatingly painful. But now, with just over a mile to go, these things didn't matter so much. Now the goal was in sight – or would have been except for the darkness; and Hooky began to feel triumphant.

'I never thought I'd do it,' he told himself, 'but I *have.* I've done it and to hell with El Vino's and the lot of them.'

The next moment he was within an ace of not completing his wager. A big black car, travelling much too fast for the narrow lane, hurtled round a bend and avoided obliterating him only by inches.

Hooky, who didn't take fright easily, was scared for the moment.

'Thank Christ for guardian angels,' he exclaimed, which for a man in whom religious feeling did not normally play a large part was unusually devout.

The big car had miraculously avoided knocking him down; but, as if in derisive contempt for anyone on foot, it had splashed him literally from top to toe with muddy water out of a wayside puddle.

In the split second in which all this had happened Hooky had caught a glimpse, registered on his retina with the sharpness of an instantaneous snapshot, of a heavy, powerful face bent over some papers in the lighted interior of the car.

The car vanished into the darkness as rapidly as it had appeared and Hooky trudged on. Presently to his infinite relief lights of the village began to appear. At first only a few scattered ones – cottages and outlying farms, he supposed; then they came more thickly, and suddenly he was at the beginning of the village street.

It occurred to him that seeing the winning post loom up at the end of the Grand National must be a feeling very much like the mixture of incredulity, triumph, infinite weariness and infinite relief which now flooded through him.

Two-thirds of the way down the street the ever blessed thing was visible. The pilgrim had now really reached Mecca. The Cobalt Arms, proclaimed the sign, and it stood outside as comfortable and decent looking a little country inn as a tired and thirsty Englishman ever set eyes on.

Charles and Martha Old had been in charge of the Cobalt Arms for fifteen years and had miraculously managed to resist nearly all modern improvements during that time. Strip-lighting, one-armed bandits and canned music had not been allowed to get a footing in the place.

'We liked it as it was when we took it over,' Mrs Old was wont to say, 'and we've done our best to keep it that way ever since.'

Martha Old was a plump, homely little person, with rosy cheeks and a woman's wise and kindly eyes; eyes which were now making shrewd assessment of the man who had just entered the tiny bar.

The Arms was always referred to as the village inn, but it would have been justified in calling itself a small hotel, for it boasted three bedrooms which did a fairly good business in the b. and b. line.

The door from the village street opened into a minute space – rather grandly referred to as 'the hall' – where Mrs Old was now sitting in what she called her office corner.

She had been going through the chore of getting the month's bills in order and the entrance of the stranger was a welcome diversion. That she smiled as soon as she set eyes on him and before ever a word was spoken was not remarkable – Hooky Hefferman, that amiable soldier of fortune, had that effect on women.

Martha Old found herself looking at a chunky-faced, muscular piece of masculinity who, if she was any judge of the world, would never be short of a bottle to drink or a woman to share it with.

What distressed her immediately was the state of his clothes.

'My word, you're all muddy!' she exclaimed. 'You *are* in a mess.'

'By courtesy of some clot in a big black car,' Hooky answered, 'and I only wish I knew who it was.'

Sir Frederick, very likely, Martha Old thought, but she kept a diplomatic silence on that probability and said instead, 'Well, we shall just have to dry you out, shan't we?'

'And what about a bed for the night?' Hooky asked anxiously.

'A bed for the night?' The slight note of hesitation in Mrs Old's voice alarmed Hooky, he was not quite sure how long his tether was, he only knew that he had come to the end of it; but the good wife continued reassuringly, 'I think we can manage that, if you don't want anything grand. We've only three rooms, the front one's being decorated; a gentleman signed into the second best only this morning; but the little one at the back is free.'

Hooky grinned hugely. 'What luck!' he exclaimed. 'Book me into the little one at the back.'

His evident relief made Martha Old smile. She had a notion that this tough-looking character would often find luck going his way in life.

Ten minutes later Hooky had been 'dried out' under Mrs Old's motherly supervision and was taken up to the little back room.

'I'm afraid it's rather simple,' was Martha Old's warning as she shut the door and left him, but in his present condition it was a simplicity that appeared almost Paradisical to Hooky.

He dumped his haversack in a corner, kicked off his shoes and stretched himself thankfully on a beautifully soft bed. His right heel felt as though it was on fire.

Above him the roof sloped down to the eaves; there was a small window across which a curtain of cottagey chintz was drawn; in one corner instead of the universal utilitarian fixed basin stood a mahogany Victorian wash-hand stand with a jug of water standing in a large white bowl; on the wall opposite him Highland cattle gazed mournfully across a cloud-wrapped glen; directly above him (he twisted round and propped himself up on one elbow to read it) a text bid him *Rest in the Lord and be content*.

During an adventurous life Hooky's direct dealings with the Lord had been minimal but if Providence had secured him this charmingly simple room in the Cobalt Arms he was profoundly grateful and well content to rest there.

An hour later he was in the hall again in search of vital information; but before he could ask his question Mrs Old pushed the hotel register towards him and invited him to sign himself in.

Only one other name had been entered that day and Hooky scanned the entry idly: *Mr R. Furlong. Caroline Crescent, Brighton. British.*

The name Furlong struck him as having pleasant rustic overtones, and dim memories from the past returned for a moment to remind him that the first great passionate love affair of his life (he was sixteen at the time) had been conducted in Brighton. These passing thoughts went out of his head almost as soon as they came in; he could hardly be expected to know that Mr R. Furlong, at the moment a name and no more, would before long become an object of the greatest interest to him.

H. Hefferman. Regency Court, Soho, London. English, Hooky wrote, and Mrs Old smiled her approval of the boldness of the handwriting and at the description of his nationality.

Duty done, Hooky asked the all-important question. Mrs Old's smile broadened. 'It's open now, Mr Hefferman,' she said. 'My husband's in there, ready to serve you.'

CHAPTER THREE

Too little care

'At our last session,' Herbert Aston said brisky, 'we were going to consider the astonishingly successful way in which Tennyson makes use of internal vowel sounds.' He reached for his pipe and began to fill it, which gave Dorothea a chance to interrupt.

'I'm sorry, Professor,' she said, 'but before we start talking about Tennyson I want to apologise.'

'Apologise?' The word surprised him. 'Whatever for?'

'At my last tutorial I'm afraid I said a lot of things that I had no right to say. I was much too outspoken and it was quite unwarranted. I apologise. I was very much moved by what you told me, but I had no right to speak as I did.'

'My dear Mrs Andrews, you had every right; in fact I think you had a duty to speak as you did.'

Dorothea Andrews could not help being amused at the little man's reaction; she thought that she had never seen him looking more alert and well pleased with things generally.

'Well, as long as you weren't upset – ' she began.

'I was profoundly upset,' the Professor cut in crisply, 'but then, you meant me to be, didn't you? Good heavens, woman. I spend hours trying to impress on you the importance of words and now you want me to believe that certain words and phrases which you used, and quite rightly used, had no real significance at all.'

'I don't mean that exactly – '

'Oh dear, I'm afraid you are going to waffle. The world is full of wafflers but I've always hoped you wouldn't turn out to be one. You didn't waffle at our last tutorial. You spoke with admirable directness. You told me what it was my duty to do.'

The remembrance that she had been bold enough to do this made Dorothea wince internally; she longed to know whether the little man had taken her advice, but she didn't like to ask.

'Do you believe in retribution?' He startled her by the question.

'Retribution?'

'You surely know what the word means,' the Professor said tartly.

'Of course I do – at least I suppose I do, I mean I suppose I know what you mean by it.'

'What I mean by it is the inevitability of life catching up with you. P. G. Wodehouse puts it splendidly somewhere. You are sailing along happily, he says, with all your ill-gotten gains in your pocket and, or so you fondly imagine, your crimes forgotten, and all the time life is waiting round the corner waiting to sock you over the head with a rubber truncheon. But then, women don't read Wodehouse much, do they?'

'*I* don't,' Dorothea answered, much amused at this revelation of a new facet of her learned tutor's character.

'A pity,' the Professor went on. 'He's full of good stuff. Most admirable verbal facilities. I don't think women read detective stories much either. Odd that. When you consider that some women write good ones. Or at any rate comparatively good; but I must say I am often distressed by the quite unnecessary stupidity with which the criminal is made to act. A little imagination would help so much.'

Dorothea didn't want the Professor to launch out – as she knew he was quite capable of doing – into a session with one of his favourite hobby-horses, she wanted to know if he had done what she told him he ought to do.

She asked him the direct question.

He hesitated for only a moment before answering, 'Yes, I went to see Maude.'

'And what happened?'

'She opened the door to me and she thought – I could see it in her eyes – how on earth did a reasonably personable young man with whom I once thought myself in love – or at any rate pretended to – how did he grow into this middle-aged uninteresting person?'

'You may be middle-aged,' Dorothea said, 'but nobody could possibly describe you as uninteresting and I won't allow you to do it either. And what did *you* think when you saw her?'

Herbert Aston drew on his pipe and watched the cloud of blue smoke which he puffed out weave itself into improbable shapes until it finally disappeared into thin air.

'When I had heard what Maude had to tell me,' he answered at length, 'I thought of Lear.'

'Lear?'

'*O, I have ta'en too little care of this* – there's something in Shakespeare to suit every occasion, to spur every laggard conscience. Shall we turn our attention to Tennyson and consider those lines towards the beginning of *The Lady of Shalott* – I expect you have committed them to memory – '

Dorothea had, and she now quoted them.

'By the margin, willow-veil'd,
Slide the heavy barges trail'd
By slow horses; and unhail'd
The shallop flitteth silken-sail'd
 Skimming down to Camelot.'

Her tutor was delighted at hearing the well-known words again and by his student's delivery of them. 'Miraculous stuff,' he said, 'miraculous. Yet what is it? Ordinary words which any one of us might have put together. Only we didn't. And it is hardly necessary to ask you to notice how magically – '

Dorothea Andrews listened partly in amusement, partly in interest to an enthusiastic disquisition on Tennyson's skilful use of internal vowel sounds ('*Can't you see those barges low in the water hardly making any perceptible progress and then the shallops coming along at lightning speed like boys skateboarding down the pavement*'). Strange little man, she thought, and she was more than ever intrigued by the glimpse she had been given into a private life which she would never have suspected. Being a woman she was something of a natural philosopher. *The truth is*, she thought, *that any man is capable of getting up to anything; you never know* . . .

At the end of the session Herbert Aston said, 'Oh, by the way, I shall be away for a few days, a week possibly. I'm going on a tour to see some of the châteaux of the Loire country.' Immediately before the tutorial he had been reading in his *Times* an advertisement of such a tour and to make use of it in this way appealed to him as a neat idea.

'Lucky you,' Dorothea said, 'that's something I would love to do.' She refrained from adding, although the thought occurred to her, that it would be a good thing for her tutor to have his mind taken off the unhappy business of his niece's suicide and all that went with it.

'So if you don't see me about for a few days don't worry,' the Professor said.

'I shall merely be envious,' Dorothea assured him, and smiled.

Herbert Aston smiled enigmatically back.

When the study door had closed behind his pupil the Professor shut and put away the Tennyson which had been lying open on the table by his chair. There was nothing phoney about his love of poetry; poetry was, and would always remain, one of the ruling forces in his life; but like many intellectuals Herbert Aston had a great opinion of himself as a man of action. He had a firm conviction that if he could be bothered to take a hand in practical matters he would have much more success in them than the so-called business magnates.

The little detail about the Loire châteaux pleased him inordinately; he didn't really think that he would need an alibi; but you never knew; meanwhile it just showed how easy it was to cover up your tracks if you wanted to, and if you gave a little thought to the matter.

The resolve had come to him after talking with Maude,

but he readily acknowledged that the origin of it lay with the pleasant woman who had just left his study and who spoke the magic words of Alfred Lord Tennyson so agreeably. It was she who, in the first place, had told him what it was his duty to do. *You must go and see her* had been the verdict. And it had been right, absolutely right. Aston acknowledged that.

And talking to Maude, listening to her story, a further and obvious duty had become clear to him.

The fact that he could now look without desire on the woman with whom he had once thought himself in love didn't lessen his feelings in the matter in the slightest. Indeed, they were strengthened by it. Herbert Aston's concern was entirely for his brother and for the memory of his brother.

Maude's story had very forcibly brought back to him memories of the long hot summers of youth and early manhood. He was willing to think now that his feelings for the girl had been naïve; but what he had felt for his brother had never been naïve, it had been deep-seated hero-worship. True his hero had acted unheroically; his god had let him down; hence twenty-eight years of estrangement and hardening of the heart; but until listening to Maude he had known nothing of Edward's tragic illness, and he had not the slightest inkling of the treatment which big business had meted out to his brother.

It was then that the accusing line from Lear had stirred in his mind, *O, I have ta'en too little care of this*. Accusing him and egging him on.

If big business had killed his brother, big business must be made to pay for it.

The hostile windmill stood up large on the horizon, and Don Quixote, who imagined himself such an adept in practical matters, conceived it to be his duty to have a tilt at it.

The châteaux of the Loire business was all nonsense, of course; but it had been fun making it up, and instructive to note how unsuspectingly it had been swallowed. Contrive a sufficiently convincing air and people tend to believe what you tell them. The thought amused the Professor. After all, he reflected, what else is the basis of conjuring, religion, medicine and, if one had to be ultimately honest, of being a professor of Eng. Lit?

Herbert Aston had no intention of going near the Loire; he was going in search of the châteaux of the Dragons of Big Business.

He stood on the narrow pavement of the City street looking up at the brazen sign VIDEX. The gilt letters looked assertive, aggressive, unyielding.

This was where, according to Maude, his dying brother Edward had come to see justice done. Justice had not been done; but possibly it had only been delayed . . .

The revolving door spun round; there was a glimpse of a uniformed commissionaire, and a man came out, hailed a passing taxi and drove off.

Matton? Aston wondered. He had no means of knowing; by now he was consumed with curiosity to find out what the dragon looked like.

Once again he studied the façade of Videx House. He was tempted to push the revolving door round and go in; but he decided to stick to the resolve he had already made: to tackle the tycoon Matton at home where he lived.

The visit to the City to look at Videx House had been made merely out of curiosity. Videx House was a stronghold; there would be commissionaires, secretaries, personal assistants and God knows what to be circumvented here, Don Quixote thought; much better stick to the plan he had already made and beard the tycoon at home where he actually lived.

He turned and made his way along the busy pavement, an inconspicuous figure in the hurrying crowd. As he went he was reflecting on something Maude had said – since their meeting certain of her words and phrases had echoed almost continually in his head – *people tend to get what they deserve*, she had said; what does the man who first of all robbed my brother and then very largely helped to kill him deserve? Herbert Aston speculated as he shouldered his way through the incurious crowd.

*

Frederick Matton stood by the dining-room window in Leys watching the drive. He took care to be partially masked by the long curtain; no point, he considered, in letting it be known that he was observing the scene. Presently the Mercedes came into view round the bushes which marked the turning to the old stable block, now the garages. It sped away towards the Lodge and the road beyond.

Matton glanced at the clock; a minute or two past one, so Tranter would be in good time picking up the prickly Donaldson. Excellent. He liked things to run to time. The thought of Donaldson troubled him for a moment. Not that the Scotsman wasn't a good accountant; he was damned good; too damned good, and, Matton was beginning to fear, getting too damned inquisitive which was why he would have to be taken care of. The visit to Paris to confer with the French auxiliary of Videx was something Matton had privately not wanted his accountant to make but he had judged it wiser not to say so.

He dismissed Donaldson from his mind; he was looking forward to a pleasant afternoon and he had no intention of spoiling it by business worries. Tranter was already conveniently out of the way and he could not possibly be back from Gatwick before half past five. Half past five was the best part of four and a half hours away. Smiling in anticipation of the agreeable afternoon before him, Matton turned away from the window and sat down to his lunch.

Lunch was followed by a cup of coffee and a cigarette, a ritual which Matton hurried slightly, for impatience was beginning to mount in him.

He selected his favourite walking stick, a heavy, silver-handled affair, from the stand in the hall and set off on foot. At a quick glance he might have been mistaken for the country squire doing the rounds of his estate; but Frederick Matton was no countryman. *Living in the country* was, as far as he was concerned, a contradiction in terms. Living for him meant the office, the City, and the daily fight that went on there with its unceasing telephone calls, cables, telex messages, luncheon talks and conspiracies.

A man had to sleep somewhere, so he had bought Leys, and having bought it his instinct was to see that it ran efficiently, either at an actual profit or at a cleverly contrived loss which would help his tax position. There were ninety-two acres in all, of which five belonged immediately to the house, the rest being farmland and woods.

It was towards the woodland that the owner of the property now made his way, first crossing the home paddock and then following for a short distance the public footpath which, much to his annoyance, ran diagonally across his land and which he had done his unsuccessful best to get closed. Matton didn't like footpaths because he didn't like the public. The public were fools, to be relieved of as much of their money as it was possible to con out of them; in that guise they were welcome; as intruders on private property they were far from welcome, they were a bloody nuisance.

Leaving the path after a hundred yards or so he came to the edge of Silverman's Wood, a mixture of beech and ash planted eighty years ago as a fox covert.

The trees in Silverman's Wood were just beginning to show signs of approaching autumn, and the afternoon sunshine filtering through the interlacing leaves made a lovely chiaroscuro of light and shade. Frederick Matton paid little attention to the incipient autumn colouring or to the play of light and shade on the woodland ride; he was impatient now to reach what lay beyond.

At the far edge of the wood, where the big twenty-two-acre field opened out, stood the hut. It had been built a full generation ago for the convenience of the shepherd in the days when the estate carried a large flock of sheep. Sheep and shepherd had long since gone, but the hut remained, convenient as a shelter for anyone caught in the rain; and convenient, as Matton had discovered, for other things too.

When he reached it no one was there.

He was not unduly put out by this. He sat down in the sunshine outside the hut to wait. *She'll come*, he told himself with conviction . . .

After a quarter of an hour he was proved right. The woman

came into view carrying a basket and walking with the springy, gypsy-like tread and the swing of the hips that appealed to him so much.

He smiled when he saw the basket, he approved of it. Always best to be on the safe side. If anyone had seen the chauffeur's wife setting out at this time of year basket in hand they would naturally think what they were meant to think – *she's off blackberrying.*

'I thought you'd be along,' Matton said.

The woman held up her basket and answered, 'I thought I'd see if I could get a few blackberries.'

Matton laughed. 'Maybe you can – after,' he said. 'He's gone to the office and after that to Gatwick so he won't be back till turned five, isn't that lucky?'

'God help us if he ever found out anything,' Molly Tranter said.

'He won't,' Matton assured her; ducking his head he went into the dark interior of the old hut and the woman followed him.

'What time is it?' The woman's voice was drowsy now and satisfied.

Matton consulted his watch. 'A quarter to four.'

'I must be going.' She rose, drew on some discarded clothes and brushed some bits of dried grass and twigs from herself.

Matton watched her lazily, feasting his eyes on her body and amused at her efforts to tidy herself up.

'Not much of a bed here, I'm afraid,' he said, 'but it serves its purpose. Any complaints?'

'Just as long as nobody knows anything,' she said. 'Roger would kill me over this.'

When she was ready to go, Matton, following their usual procedure, said, 'Just a minute whilst I make sure no one's about.'

He stood in the doorway of the hut and looked around. He thought it highly unlikely that he would see anybody and in fact he did not do so.

He moved back into the hut.

'O.K. Better pick a few blackberries on the way home. Give Roger some for his supper; he may as well have something to enjoy.'

She smiled her gypsy-like smile at him and went out basket in hand. Matton lit a cigarette and waited for the customary safety interval to give her time to get well clear.

After five minutes he himself emerged from the hut and, stick in hand, started on his way back through Silverman's Wood. His mood was the masculine one of post-coital content with the world; he vaguely remembered reading about a Frenchman, a poet or painter or something of that sort, who notched his walking stick every time he had a conquest. *By God,* he thought with a laugh, *I'd have to cut a damned good notch today –*

'Excuse me.'

He was startled; thoroughly startled. Who the hell was this? he wondered, and where the hell had he come from? And, much more to the point, how long had he been there?

Matton gave a rapid backward glance. The hut was barely fifty yards away, its entrance still only too clearly visible. Had he been careful enough when looking out for possible danger? He didn't like this situation at all.

'What are you doing here?' he asked.

'I'm afraid I have rather lost my way. There was a clearly marked footpath at one point but I seem to have got off it.'

'You're right off it. You're trespassing.'

'Oh dear. This wood is private then, is it?'

'It belongs to Sir Frederick Matton.'

'Ah, I thought it might. Do you happen to know him?'

'I work for him.'

'I suppose he'll be down for the weekend, will he? That's what I'm banking on.'

'He's usually here at weekends, yes. Why?'

'I hope to have the very doubtful pleasure of calling on the gentleman tomorrow.'

Matton studied the stranger in silence for a few seconds, considering. He wasn't sure what to do for the best.

'How long had you been hanging about before you spoke to me?' he asked at last.

'Hanging about?' The trespasser laughed. 'I wouldn't call that a very complimentary phrase.'

Matton wanted to ask him if he had seen anybody coming out of the old hut; but he didn't like to; he judged the question to be dangerous. For all he knew the whole situation might be dangerous. He wondered what tomorrow would bring forth; meanwhile he was giving nothing away today.

'If you take my advice,' he said, 'you'll get back on to the footpath and stick to it.'

'My husband's in there waiting to serve you,' Martha Old said reassuringly and Hooky thought that he had seldom heard words of greater comfort and cheer.

Hooky Hefferman was not a great Italian scholar, but he knew the famous quotation from Dante and in his opinion it should appear, in slightly altered form, over the entrance to every saloon bar: 'Renew your hope all ye who enter here.'

Certainly, he decided at once, it should be written up over the entrance to the small, warm, polished place he now went into. Hooky was a pub man, a connoisseur of the thing, and what the Cobalt Arms had to offer scored an instant bull with him.

'Good evening, sir,' Charles Old welcomed him from behind the bar. The landlord had already had a potted account of the new occupant of the small back room from his wife, and was interested to see the man who could make such a favourable impression in so short a time. What he saw didn't disappoint him; he agreed with his wife as he very frequently did. He liked the look of this cheerful soldier of fortune. And Hooky in his turn liked what he saw: he approved on sight of the short, rotund figure who looked affable, polite and discreet. Not for the first time in his life Hooky reflected that if the Cabinet consisted entirely of successful publicans the affairs of the country would be infinitely better managed than they are.

'What can I get for you, sir?'

'A vital question,' Hooky said, running his eye along the splendidly well-stocked shelves and positively wallowing in the masochistic pleasure of deliberately drawn-out anticipation.

'An Odyssey has been completed,' he explained. 'In the last seven days I have performed prodigies of valour and endurance. I must have something sustaining, invigorating and sufficiently noble to serve as a celebration of a great occasion – ' He broke off these admirable introductory remarks because his glance had fallen on a faded photograph pinned up behind the bar.

A photograph of a house; and, to Hooky's surprise, a photograph of a house that he knew.

'Isn't that Great Keeling Hall?' he asked.

'That's right, sir. Do you know it?'

'I visited it once as a boy.'

'Did you indeed, sir?' Old was delighted and not in the least surprised; he had already formed the opinion that Hooky, even if he did look a trifle battered, came out of the right stable. 'I started my service life as page-boy in that house, sir. Thirteen years old and thirteen ball buttons down the front of my waistcoat and didn't they just have to be polished every day. My word, what a different world it was! Wellington Barracks wasn't in it the way that house was run. We grumbled a bit, of course, but couldn't we all do with a touch of it now. A proper Tartar she was, the lady of the house. Mrs Page-Foley. One of the old sort, a real old dragon.'

'My aunt,' Hooky said.

The landlord's delight was increased. 'Is that so, sir? Well, I *am* pleased to meet you. Is the old lady still alive?'

'Alive and kicking,' Hooky assured him, 'and terrorising a large section of the population of Hove. She'll be alive when the Day of Judgement comes, that one; and God help Gabriel if he blows a wrong note on his trumpet.'

Old laughed. 'Well, this is a real red-letter day,' he said, 'meeting somebody who knew the old house. What was it you said you wanted to drink, sir – something invigorating and sustaining and by way of a celebration?'

'A bottle of Moët & Chandon wouldn't come amiss.'

'Ah, I think we can do better than that, sir. That's what I should call *ordinary* celebration; I've got something in the cellar just a bit *extra*ordinary, just right for such an occasion as this; if you'll excuse me a minute, sir – '

The landlord disappeared from sight and Hooky looked round the bar. Only one other devotee was in the temple and he did not appear to be in festive mood. Dressed in the anonymous garb of grey flannel trousers and sports jacket, he sat some distance away, thin-faced and sardonic of aspect. But Hooky was buoyed up on the waves of euphoria; the triumphal ending of his great adventure so rashly entered into in El Vino's induced him to view the world and all its inhabitants through rose-tinted glasses.

'Have you ever walked one hundred and fifty miles in seven days?' he enquired.

'I wouldn't be such a damned fool,' the sardonic one answered. 'What are motor-cars for?'

'The internal-combustion engine was invented,' Hooky assured him, 'for the express purpose of cracking civilisation.'

'Is that your opinion?' the man asked, adding, 'And I expect you've got a nice large Rolls-Royce tucked away in your garage in the commuter belt all the time.'

'Now then, sir,' said Charles Old, emerging through a trap-door in the floor behind the bar like a character in the old pantomime, 'I've got something here as *is* something.'

With reverential care he placed three bottles on the counter and with due solemnity spoke to Hooky about them.

'That's Coronation Barley Wine, Mr Hefferman, that is; brewed way back in 1952 the year Her Majesty, God bless her, came to the throne. My word, the service that woman has given to this country in twenty-five years! That was made strong when they brewed it and it's got stronger every year since. That's none of your cat-lap stuff, that's the genuine article that is. When I came here to the Arms I brought two dozen bottles with me and I've still got a dozen left. I keep it for very special occasions and I reckon this *is* a very special occasion, meeting a gentleman as knew the old house, especially a nephew of Mrs Page-Foley.'

Any lingering regrets that Hooky might have entertained at not being ministered to by his favourite doctors Messrs Moët & Chandon disappeared as the first tentative sips of the golden liquid began to do their magical work. Tidings of great joy were carried to every part of his body; he felt as though men with lighted torches were speeding through his veins touching off bonfires of celebration and delight. It was impossible not to speak of the miraculous discovery to someone.

'By God,' he avowed, 'it was worth every yard of a hundred and fifty miles to find this marvellous stuff.'

The man in the sports jacket showed no signs even of vicarious enthusiasm. 'All right if you can afford it,' he said. 'I can't. Not on the pay they give me for my job.'

'You ought to be in my profession,' Hooky told him, laughing. 'I very often do a hell of a lot of work and don't get paid at all.'

'More fool you. What line are you in, then?'

Hooky took another mouthful of the Coronation Brew and was instantly confirmed in his recently formed view that the world was an excellent place and all the people in it excellent fellows.

'I am a private investigator,' he announced with dignity. 'Confidential missions and enquiries of every sort undertaken. Secrecy and promptness guaranteed.'

'You're pulling my leg; you're joking.'

'Indeed I am not,' Hooky assured him. 'If you find yourself in any sort of trouble, the odd murder or a spot of blackmail, anything of that kind, just apply to the old firm and all will be well – for a consideration, of course.'

The man stared at him incredulously. 'You really mean to tell me,' he demanded, 'that you are one of these so-called Private Eyes?'

Hooky admitted that that was the information he had been trying to convey. The other man rose and made preparations to depart. 'Well, you live and learn,' he said morosely. 'I never thought I'd meet one. Not in the flesh. All this nonsense on TV and in the paperbacks is bad enough, but to think I'd ever come across one of the crackpots in reality! Take my tip, Mister Confidential Investigator or whatever you call yourself, and leave catching villains to people who can catch them, to the law.'

Hooky laughed as the door closed; the beatific influence of twenty-five-year-old Coronation Brew was making him too happy to feel any annoyance.

'Not exactly a ray of sunshine, is he?' was his mild comment.

'Ah, you don't want to take no notice of Harry West,' the landlord told him. 'Mind you, I've got to, up to a point. There's always my licence to think about. Harry's the local policeman. He's good at his job, I'll give him that; but you couldn't call him popular. He's too clever and he's too sarky. He looks in here occasionally when he's off duty; well, why shouldn't he? A bobby's entitled to his pint same as anybody else.'

Hooky nodded agreement. 'All the same, I wouldn't make a pet of him,' he said.

The barley wine was dealt with slowly and lovingly. Hooky was sure that the gods merely sipped their nectar, and equally sure that no nectar ever tasted better than the mirage-invoking stuff which landlord Old had magic-ed up out of his cellar. The normal traffic of a quiet evening went on; there were one or two incursions of passing trade; the local habitués came in for their ritual sustenance against the slings and arrows; there was no juke-box, no one-armed bandit, only the quiet, reverential hush proper to a temple. There was ample time for the landlord and Hooky to converse.

'Have you met the other gentleman staying with us, sir?'

Hooky had not yet done so.

'A Mr Furlong. Very quiet, he seems. Very pleasant. Says he has come here for two or three days to do some bird-watching.'

Hooky said he himself had done a certain amount of bird-watching in his time, but probably it was of a different sort.

Old laughed. 'I can believe that, Mr Hefferman,' he said, 'but there you are – the ladies, God bless 'em, what should we do without them?'

'Get ourselves into all sorts of trouble,' Hooky assured him, 'and it wouldn't be half so satisfactory; we shouldn't know which way to turn.'

He considered his bottle, which was now empty.

'The Lamp of Inspiration languishes for lack of oil,' he pointed out. 'A quotation from Mr Chu-Ling, a Chinese philosopher of discernment and wisdom.'

'We never entertained any Chinese gentlemen at the Hall,' Old said, 'but there's no cause for the lamp to go out, Mr Hefferman; I brought three bottles up from the cellar and I don't reckon to take any back. I don't believe in going backwards.'

'Forward the tight brigade,' Hooky agreed. 'A very admirable sentiment.' He reached for the second bottle.

'Do you see anything of your aunt these days?' Old asked.

'As little as possible,' Hooky told him. 'It's a very hazardous occupation is visiting my aunt.'

'Hove, did you say she's living at, sir?'

'In the deserts of flat-land when the mournful cry of three-no-trumps echoes dismally across the arid wastes of afternoon.'

It was not a busy evening and there was no one else with Hooky when the other visitor to the Arms came in. Being of a gregarious nature Hooky was glad to see him; any company was better than none, and the bird-watching character seemed a harmless and agreeable type.

'Any luck in the woods?' Hooky greeted him. 'Any blue-throated turn-turds or similar excitements?'

Herbert Aston was at a loss for a moment, then he remembered that he had said something about bird-watching; he was thoroughly enjoying the business of building up a false personality for himself, but he was apt to forget his lines now and again.

'You didn't go anywhere near Sweeting Bog, did you, Mr Furlong?' Old asked anxiously.

'Sweeting Bog?'

'I ought to have warned you about it, but I never thought to because all of us round here know it so well. It lies about two miles the other side of the village, where the common lands used to be according to the old chaps; and you want to give it a miss; it's a dangerous place is Sweeting Bog.'

'I didn't see any sign of it,' Aston said, 'but I did lose my way at one point. I was on a footpath and it suddenly petered out.'

'The footpaths aren't kept up like they used to be,' the landlord agreed. 'People don't walk so much these days for one thing, and then Sir Frederick isn't keen on footpaths, anyway.'

'Would that be Sir Frederick Matton?'

'That's it, sir. Lives at the big house. Leys they call it. Well, I say *lives* there; it's only partly true; he's up in London most of the time making money; he doesn't live in the place in the way the old-fashioned village squire used to do.'

'Is he popular?'

Charles Old smiled diplomatically. 'If I was to start talking village gossip in the Arms that would never do,' he said. 'I should get into plenty of trouble that way. You haven't said what you would like to drink yet, sir.'

In his best professional tones Aston said that he would like a small dry Sercial.

Hooky, who took a vicarious interest in what anybody drank, looked on benignly. He had nothing whatever against Sercial; there had been times when a small dry Sercial would have seemed very desirable, but tonight it sounded like the feeble spluttering of a match compared to the splendid illumination going on inside himself.

'Does this person Matton employ a gamekeeper?' Aston asked. 'Would that be the man who told me I was trespassing?'

'I expect that would be Roger Tranter,' the landlord guessed. 'He's really the chauffeur, but he does a bit of keepering and acts as a sort of bodyguard in a way. You know what these rich men are, they want someone to come between them and the rest of us; they want to keep the world at bay.'

'An exercise in which they are not always successful,' Herbert Aston said; he took a sip of his dry Sercial and rolled it appreciatively round his palate before adding quietly, 'Things have a habit of catching up with people, even with very rich people, sometimes.'

CHAPTER FOUR

Fifty thousand pounds

Frederick Matton was looking forward to the interview with curiosity. Any man who, one way or another, has amassed a fortune of several millions must reconcile himself to being an obvious target for all sorts of religious fanatics, do-gooders, cranks, spongers and just plain beggars.

Matton was used to this hazard; it was largely to deal with nuisances of this sort that he employed a tough, strong-arm character like Roger Tranter. The chauffeur-game-keeper-bodyguard understood his position perfectly and enjoyed fulfilling it.

In this particular instance Matton said nothing to his chauffeur about the visitor he was expecting; he had thought hard about the encounter in Silverman's Wood and had come to the optimistic conclusion that in all probability the stranger, whoever he was, had not been there when Mollie actually came out of the hut and had seen nothing of her; but it was just as well to be on the safe side, and it was clearly better not to bring Tranter into the business at all. Matton had no illusions about Roger Tranter. The chauffeur had been inside once on a charge of G.B.H. and if he lost his temper about anything he would be only too ready to inflict G.B.H. again.

Meanwhile, if the man who had spoken to him in the wood turned out to be the usual thing – a hard-luck story or some crackpot inventor with a crazy idea – Matton felt confident of being able to deal with him – yet was he going to turn out to be the usual thing? Matton had some doubts about it. A first glance gave you the impression that the stranger was rather insignificant, but somehow on a second look and when you heard him speak you felt inclined to revise this opinion; and then there had been the rather strange wording he had used, '. . . I hope to have the doubtful pleasure of calling on the gentleman tomorrow.'

The butler came into the room. 'A Mr Furlong wants to see you, Sir Frederick. Shall I tell him you are not at home?'

'No, show him in.'

Herbert Aston came in and was taken aback.

'Are you Frederick Matton?' he asked.

'I am.' The big man smiled complacently at his visitor's discomfort.

'You didn't say so yesterday in the wood.'

'You never asked me. That's one point. Another point is that you had no right to be in the wood, let alone ask questions of its owner. But now that you know who I am, may I ask who you are? I don't think I know anyone of the name of Furlong.'

'Neither do I. Does the word Notas mean anything to you?'

So much had happened since the early days, there had been so many legal complications, such a multitude of changes, alterations, corrections and revisions that Matton had quite genuinely forgotten the original name of the invention which ultimately made a fortune for him.

'Notas?' he queried. For a moment he was at a loss, then memory clicked and he looked at his visitor with fresh interest. 'Yes, I have heard the word,' he said. 'What about it?'

'It's an anagram of my brother's name. Aston. Edward Aston. I am Edward Aston's brother.'

'So what? What am I supposed to say? Pleased to meet you, Mr Aston?'

The visitor smiled. He found himself enjoying the man-of-action role which he had undertaken. 'I don't think you will be in the least pleased,' he replied. 'I hope not, anyway. My brother invented something out of which you made a fortune. He made next to nothing. I want to put that right.'

Matton sighed; the weary sigh of a man bored at the prospect of having to explain matters from the beginning to somebody who probably wouldn't understand them anyway. He drew a silver box towards him and took out a fat, hand-made Turkish cigarette. He offered one to his visitor who refused it with an impatient gesture.

'Are you a business man, Mr Aston?'

'I am *not*. I have managed to make my living comparatively honestly so far.'

'You are a scientist or inventor perhaps?'

'I know absolutely nothing about science or machinery of any kind. I'm a believer in justice.'

'And you don't think anybody else believes in it, I suppose?'

'I don't think *you* do. You managed to get hold of something my brother had invented and made a fortune out of it; he died in poverty.'

'And are you suggesting that I'm responsible for that?'

'Certainly.'

Matton laughed. 'Nothing like speaking your mind,' he said. 'By the way, when did your brother die?'

'Just over eighteen years ago.'

'It has taken a long time for this famous sense of justice of yours to function, hasn't it?'

'I quarrelled with my brother more than twenty-eight years ago. He did something which I thought dishonourable and we ceased to have anything to do with one another; but the other day something happened which made me look into his affairs a little.'

'What was that?'

'His eighteen-year-old daughter committed suicide.'

'And I suppose I'm responsible for that?'

'In a way, yes, I think you are.'

Matton laughed again, more harshly this time. 'My God,' he said, 'you busybodies have got a nerve. Suppose you belt up for a minute or so and listen to a few facts instead of spouting all this woolly idealistic stuff you seem to have got hold of.

'Notas. Yes, I know all about Notas now, of course I do; far more than you ever will, or ever could by the sound of you. There was a firm in the South of England, somewhere in Sussex, called Oxtone Limited – all this is years ago, by the way. Oxtone had been badly run; it was pathetically under-financed and generally in a mess. In fact the concern was on its way out. But it did have potential. If somebody was willing to risk over a million pounds and put in months and months of hard work there was just a chance of pulling things round and making it a viable affair.

'I was willing to risk the money and put in the hard work; but I suppose you've got something to say against that, have you?'

'What about my brother's idea, his invention?'

'Your brother's invention was part of the firm, part of Oxtone Limited. And, incidentally, it was in a pretty elementary form; it needed a hell of a lot of development before we made it into a real success.'

'But the idea was his.'

'Until we bought it. Or don't you believe in buying and selling? Perhaps you don't believe in private property; perhaps that's why you were trespassing on my property yesterday.'

'I started off on a public footpath.'

'A pity you didn't stay on it.'

'Is that hut yours as well?'

Matton paused for a moment and then asked, 'What hut?'

'I saw some sort of hut at the edge of the wood.'

'And what has it got to do with you whose hut it is?'

'Nothing whatever. I was merely being curious.'

'Will you let a poor, ignorant business man give you a piece of advice, Aston? I should stop being curious if I were you, curiosity can be dangerous.'

'Are you threatening me? I find that amusing.'

'Do you? Well, shall we stop the cross-talk and get back to plain facts. This Oxtone outfit was on its last legs and if I hadn't bought it up it would have sunk without trace.'

'But you made a fortune out of it.'

'You keep saying that as though to make money is some sort of crime; how do you imagine old-age pensions and social security and all the rest of it is paid for? Where does the money for all that come from if it doesn't come out of taxing the people who have made a bit?'

'I don't want a lesson on economics from you, Matton.'

'What do you want?'

'I want fifty thousand pounds.'

Matton laughed. 'Do you indeed?' he asked.

'And that won't really make up for all the harm that has been done – my brother's death and his daughter's suicide.'

'Be your age, for God's sake. People work out their own tragedies, I'm not responsible for them. What were you doing to help your brother, anyway?'

'Nothing. That's why I'm here now. Apparently when Edward went to see you – and he got up out of hospital to do it – you told him that you had never even heard of Notas.'

'That's his account of things.'

'I believe it.'

'Do you? And it's only five minutes ago you were telling me that this brother of yours did something so dishonourable that you packed up and had nothing to do with him for years. As a matter of fact, at that time Notas hardly existed. I've just told you, the Sussex firm was in such a mess hardly anything existed in any viable sense. Everything had to be rescued, developed, financed; and I can tell you it cost me one hell of a lot of money to do it.'

'It cost Edward his life and his daughter hers, and now I want you to make recompense to his widow. I want you to pay her fifty thousand pounds.'

Matton reached forward to stub out his cigarette in a heavy glass ash-tray. He performed the action deliberately, taking time over it. Time during which he considered a number of things. He couldn't be sure how much this troublesome brother of Edward Aston's really knew; the take-over of the Sussex firm had not been without some dubious aspects and Videx certainly didn't want the whole business revived and possibly taken into the courts. Did the widow possess any signed agreements or letters which this meddlesome brother had unearthed and which might prove awkward? Fifty thousand pounds was nonsense, of course. Blackmail. But was it worth while offering a completely ex-gratia payment to the widow of, say, five thousand? Or would that be dangerous? Was this blasted brother likely to go with his story to a Sunday newspaper and what would happen to Videx shares if they ran it as a big business scandal? And, perhaps even more to the point, how much had this trespasser in the woods really seen of the hut and who came out of it?

Matton watched the last vestige of smoke coming from his now squashed cigarette end and decided that it would be best to have a word with the firm's lawyer and it might even be necessary to bring Donaldson into it.

He felt furious with the interfering little man who had popped up from nowhere and made such a nuisance of himself, but when he finally spoke he schooled his voice to sound reasonable. 'Fifty thousand pounds is a great deal of money,' he said. 'I expect you realise that there can be no question of a sum like that. And please understand that I am not admitting any liability whatsoever. No liability exists. I am prepared, however, to think the matter over and to see if anything can be done. But you must give me a little time. I suggest that you leave your address with me and go back home, and you will hear from me in a very short time.'

Herbert Aston rose. 'Delaying tactics,' he said. 'I expected them. Reasonable up to a point, I suppose. You say that no obligation exists. Except, I would point out, the obligation of honour and justice. I happen to be a believer in justice, Matton, so don't delay your answer long. And I shan't bother to go home, I find I am very comfortable at the Cobalt Arms.'

The Paris meeting was held in the showy Videx offices in the huge modern building just off the rue Didot. Things went much as Donaldson expected them to. He said his piece; he was asked his opinion three or four times; he listened while the chairman talked.

It all went smoothly – too smoothly? Donaldson couldn't help wondering. Once or twice he caught the eye of the American, a thin, dark man with the nicotine-stained fingers of the heavy chain-smoker. The business came to an end; the chairman made the usual polite little speech of dismissal; people began to put their papers away in brief-cases, to go in search of hats and coats. Nicotine-stained fingers touched Donaldson on the arm and he turned.

'Doing anything? Busy?' the American asked, and when Donaldson shook his head he went on, 'Let's go back to my hotel, shall we, and see if we can't rustle up something to drink.'

They walked the short distance to the rue de Clery and went into a modest-looking building that faced the street with a somewhat dingy front. A front which was belied by the inside, which was clean and comfortable.

'Not one of the swagger-places,' the American said, 'but it suits me. I leave the swagger-places to the swagger-boys; and I dislike 'em both just about equally.'

He ordered drinks and whilst waiting for them to be brought there were a few moments of awkward silence. Donaldson wondered why the man had brought him there.

The drinks came and the American raised his glass. 'Here's luck,' he said. 'We shall both need it.'

He jerked his head to indicate the place they had recently come from. 'What did you think of it?' he asked.

'More or less routine, wasn't it?' Donaldson said, and the other man laughed. 'Seen that bastard Matton lately?' he asked.

Donaldson smiled a little wryly and said, 'The trouble is I see rather too much of him.'

'I wouldn't let that worry you.'

What the hell is that supposed to mean? the accountant wondered; he took stock of the man sitting opposite him, thin fingers wrapped round the tall glass, a lock of black hair falling untidily across the sallow face. Donaldson didn't know much about the American and had never been entirely clear as to his position in the company. Something on the technical side; and always with a faint air of hush-hush and mystery about him.

'I don't think you'll be seeing so much of Matton in the future.'

The remark astonished Donaldson; the possibility of the head of Videx resigning had never entered his reckoning. 'You don't mean to tell me he's thinking of resigning?' he said.

That made the American laugh; he crooked his finger for the waiter to take the empty glasses away and recharge them. He drew a yellow packet from his pocket and extracted a thin, abnormally long cigarette from it. He took time in lighting the cigarette and then watched the smoke spiralling up towards the ceiling. Finally he spoke.

'No,' he said, 'I don't. His sort don't resign; they scuttle the bloody ship and everybody else in it and get themselves picked up nice and comfortable in a God-damn helicopter and whirled off to some place else. What was the phrase your chaps had during the war? F—— you, Jack, I'm all right. That's Matton's philosophy.'

The waiter brought the drinks and the American indicated for them to be put on his bill.

He raised his glass. 'Well, here's luck again,' he said, 'like I told you, it looks as though we shall need it.'

Donaldson was fully alerted now. 'Why? What's going to happen?' he asked.

The American took a mouthful of drink and drew on his long cigarette.

'I know what's going to happen as far as I'm concerned,' he said. 'I'm sending in my resignation tonight.' He tapped his breast pocket. 'I've got it written out already. I'm not going to let Matton have the pleasure of ditching me.'

'Ditching you? Is there any talk of ditching you?'

The thin face creased into a sour smile.

'Only behind my back. And behind yours, too.'

'Mine?'

'That's why I suggested we had this talk together.'

Donaldson stared at the man; he didn't know what to make of what he was being told. Or half told. He began to remember a number of small things which he hadn't liked but which, at the time, hadn't seemed worth bothering about.

The American very carefully tapped the ash off his cigarette into the glass ash-tray. When this operation had been performed with great deliberation, he said:

'Matton is going to cut Videx in two. Right down the middle. Like slicing an apple in two. And the half he doesn't want he's going to throw away. Into the trash-bin. Finish. And that means you and me. Our two names are on the throw-away list.'

'He can't do that to me,' Donaldson protested. 'He can't sack me like that.'

'Why not?' the American laughed. 'He's the boss.'

'But I've put years into the firm. I've helped to build it up. Matton owes a hell of a lot to me.'

'And you think he cares about that?'

'He must do. He can't mean just to give me notice and throw me out.'

'He can't?'

From his right-hand side pocket the American produced a buff-coloured envelope; out of the envelope he drew a folded sheet of paper. He unfolded it and laid it on the table, smoothing it flat with thin fingers. It was a piece of Videx office memorandum paper. What was on it was written in handwriting which the accountant knew and recognised beyond any possibility of doubt. It was a detailed, unmistakable blueprint for ruthless hatchet work. Dates were mentioned and names. Donaldson read his own name there.

He read the astonishing document through twice, very slowly and his mind was in a turmoil . . .

CHAPTER FIVE

Lest we lose our Edens

Hooky was engaged in easy and agreeable conversation with Charles Old. The landlord was delighted that his visitor had decided to prolong his stay at the Arms for two or three days. Hooky's immediate excuse for this decision was a large and painful blister on his right heel, but even without that very valid reason he would have been tempted to stay on. The simple truth was that he liked the place; he liked Martha and Charles Old; and seen from a distance the clutter and clatter of Soho was singularly unattractive. Hooky, it's true, was essentially a metropolitan animal, but all animals are better for being out at grass now and again.

'Takes me right back to old times, Mr Hefferman,' Old said, 'talking to you and thinking about your aunt.'

Hooky closed his eyes for a moment. 'My dear old inn-keeper,' he said, 'why let your mind run on morbid subjects? It's a nice day, let us concentrate on all things bright and beautiful.'

Old laughed. 'And the Colonel,' he went on. 'A proper fiery old gentleman! Your aunt was the only one as could keep him in order.'

Hooky gave it as his opinion that his aunt would keep an earthquake in order.

'I expect you know about the time he shot the barometer?'

Hooky was mildly surprised. 'I know the old boy was in the habit of slaughtering lots of pheasants and partridges,' he said. 'In fact I suppose any living thing on the estate had a pretty thin time one way or another; and no doubt a keeper or two got peppered occasionally; but I never knew barometers were included in the bag.'

'Ah, this was different, sir. Haymaking time this was.

What was called the Little Paddock, close to the Hall, where the hunters used to be turned out. Only this time it was being kept for hay. There was a big, old-fashioned barometer used to hang just inside the front door. The Colonel tapped it every time he went by it. Which, incidentally, made Mrs Page-Foley cross. "Never tap a barometer," she kept telling him, "it's quite wrong." Well, when it came time for cutting the hay in the Little Paddock naturally the Colonel was watching the barometer and tap-tap-tapping the poor thing constantly for the best part of two days.

'It kept going up and pointing to *Fine and Dry*, so the orders went out from G.H.Q. (that's what the staff always called the Colonel's study) that it was to be haymaking to-morrow.

'Three of the gardeners were warned and a man from the stables; and of course the Colonel himself was going to be there to direct operations.

'Directly after breakfast next morning (and breakfast *was* breakfast in those days, Mr Hefferman; what the Colonel liked was a nice bit of rare steak with a fried egg on top of it), well, like I say, directly after breakfast everybody began to get ready and no sooner were they all got together than the heavens opened and the rain fairly poured down.

'The Colonel rushed into the hall and looked at the barometer. According to him it still said *Fine and Dry*; anyway, he tore it off the wall and ran outside with it.

' "See for yourself, you bloody stupid thing," he shouted and he put it up on one of the wrought-iron garden benches and shot it to pieces.'

'An act typical of a man in his position,' was the comment of P.C. West who had come into the bar in time to hear the gist of the anecdote.

The police constable was in uniform, and he carried in his hand the reason of his visit – a coloured poster.

'If you wouldn't mind putting this up in the bar, Mr Old,' he said. 'We're supposed to get as many round as we can – Colorado beetles.'

'And what have they been up to?' Hooky enquired jovially. 'Mayhem and so on?'

'Ah, naturally you smart Private Investigators wouldn't know about things like Colorado beetles. No glamour in it. My God, where's the glamour in sheep scab, fowl pest and swine fever?'

Hooky said he honestly couldn't think of three less glamorous subjects.

'Of course you can't. That's why you leave 'em alone. I can't leave 'em alone. I'm just an ordinary overworked, underpaid policeman. Fetch and carry. Come and go. Do as I'm told. At the orders of my superior officers. And, my word, the way they carry on. This colonel you've been talking about who shot the barometer – I'll bet he was a magistrate, sat on the local bench, didn't he?'

'Actually he was one of the fetch and carry, come and go, do as you're told brigade,' Hooky said. 'He was married to my aunt.'

When the policeman had gone Old made a humorously apologetic face at Hooky.

'What did I tell you, Mr Hefferman?' he said. 'Harry's one of the awkward sort. He's got this chip on his shoulder because he hasn't got any stripes on his arm. You don't want to let him worry you.'

Hooky said that in such a pleasant spot as the village of Sweeting and with a long, untroubled session in the bar of the Cobalt Arms in prospect he hadn't the slightest intention of letting anything worry him, 'All the same,' he added, 'I wouldn't like to be a Colorado beetle and have that disgruntled copper chasing after me.'

The next visitor to enter the bar was no disgruntled copper, but somebody much more to Hooky's taste.

She was dark and, although not specifically pretty, there was something striking and even compelling about her features. The stamp of being essentially a woman, a female animal, was very strong upon her. No man could mistake it. She walked with a hint of springiness in her step as a gypsy might.

'And what can I get for you, Mollie?' Old enquired.

The woman said that she wanted a bottle of sherry to take home with her.

'It's the sweet kind you like, isn't it?'

'That's right, Mr Old.'

Whilst the landlord went to his storeroom to get the bottle of sherry the woman and Hooky took frank stock of one another. What Hooky found himself looking at was something he had seen more often than was good for him up and down the world, in all sorts of likely and unlikely places – a delectable, dangerous man-trap, to be avoided at all costs by prudent people – but how could a man be bothered with prim prudence when on holiday, with a hundred and fifty meritorious miles behind him and a huge blister on his right heel to prove it?

What the woman found herself looking at, with fully comprehending eyes, made her smile, slowly and tentatively.

Hooky took encouragement from that smile.

'Do me a favour,' he asked.

'A favour?'

'I hate drinking alone – '

'You needn't,' she assured him. 'I should like a large gin and tonic.'

The landlord returned and was not much surprised to receive the order; being of the old regime he subscribed to the belief that a gentleman should never run away from danger.

Twenty pleasant minutes later the woman laughingly told Hooky that skilled though he was at blandishments she was not going to be induced to have yet another drink and she must be hurrying away home.

'You leave me desolate,' Hooky said.

'You'll recover,' she told him. 'Your sort always do.'

In the doorway she collided with the second visitor to the Arms. Mollie Tranter didn't in the least mind being bumped into by a man; but for a second or two the newcomer was slightly embarrassed. He dropped the book he was carrying and by the time he had recovered it the woman, with a laughing half apology ('Sorry, I wasn't looking'), had gone. She had never seen Herbert Aston before and couldn't have cared less who he was; but he had seen her once and he wondered very much who she might be.

Hooky, always avid of company, was delighted to see him.

'How's the bird-watching?' he enquired genially. 'Any spotted bottlenecks about?'

Aston smiled; he already liked this amiable extrovert, and he was feeling elated. The way he had conducted his interview with Frederick Matton seemed extremely satisfactory to him, and altogether he was well pleased with his success in his assumed role. He was about to order himself a drink when he was forestalled.

'A small dry Sercial for Mr Furlong,' Hooky said, 'and a large wet Pimms for me.'

Aston watched the preparation of the Pimms with interest but presently betrayed what his thoughts were by asking, 'Who was that lady going out just as I came in?'

Old turned the query over in his mind; it's a topsy-turvy world, right enough, he thought. Chauffeurs' wives are ladies now; cleaning women are charladies; everyone is a lady nowadays, except often enough those who should be, and who only too frequently don't act up to the part.

Hooky was also curious to know who the man-trap was, but with the usual self-confidence of the successful male he felt it incumbent upon himself to warn the obviously innocent.

'When the apple reddens
never pry
Lest we lose our Edens
Eve and I,'

he quoted.

Aston was delighted. 'Browning,' he said. 'I wouldn't have thought that you read much of him.'

'Bits stick,' Hooky said, almost apologetically, 'especially bits from old Chi-Lung – he who walks in the jungle will one day meet a tiger, the old Chink said; and by tiger he really meant, of course, tigress; which is naturally worse; the female of the species and so on. My advice, based on a certain amount of experience, is give tigresses a miss.'

Herbert Aston took an appreciative sip of his Sercial and said in his best professional tones, 'I seldom ask other people's advice and never take it.'

Hooky was amused with the reply; and it struck him once again that there was more quality about the little bird-watcher than might appear at first sight.

From behind the bar Old supplied information. 'That was Mrs Tranter, that was,' he said. 'Roger Tranter's wife.'

'Roger Tranter? Didn't you tell me that he is chauffeur to this man Matton?'

'That's right, sir.'

'And that lady is his wife?'

'She is, sir.'

'Indeed, how very interesting.'

Hooky wondered what it was about that particular item of information that was of such interest.

'And how do Roger Tranter and his good-looking wife get on together?' Aston asked.

The question shocked Charles Old; by his standards it was not one which should have been asked in the bar of the Arms; he certainly had no intention of discussing the private affairs of his customers.

'I wouldn't know anything about that, Mr Furlong,' he said. 'That's their affair, that is.'

The implied rebuke seemed to go unnoticed.

'She looked a very lively person to me,' Aston said. 'I suppose she gets left alone a lot, with her husband chauffeur-ing all over the place?'

Hooky heard this with dismay. We never learn, he thought, none of us. Why the hell can't this nice little guy be content with watching his chuff-chiffs or whatever they are and leave other men's wives alone? I'll bet my bottom dollar he can't swim a yard and yet he looks like taking a header into the deep end. Why don't we all keep our flies permanently zipped up?

'Have another Sercial,' he suggested, 'and remember Chi-Lung.'

'Another Sercial? Yes, I think I will. I usually restrict myself to one, but this is turning out to be an occasion. Quite an occasion; and with regard to your Chinese philosopher friend I've already told you my reaction to advice given me by other people.'

Silently Hooky pushed two empty glasses across the bar; he caught the landlord's eye and they exchanged glances.

The woman with the gypsy-like walk went home to Lodge Cottage carrying her bottle of sweet sherry. Like many highly sexed women she was not a heavy drinker and did not often touch spirits, but she liked her glass of sweet sherry.

On her way home through the village she met a couple of women she knew. The civilities that passed between them were of the briefest kind. Mollie Tranter didn't have much time for women, and she was well aware, and indeed gratified by the fact, that other women didn't have much time for her. Instinct warned them of danger.

She had lived in Sweeting for nearly two years and didn't like the place. 'I am not a village person,' she was in the habit of avowing; but during the last few months things had taken a turn which made living there an exciting business. Exciting but dangerous; exciting because dangerous. She had to be very, very careful with Roger. Just before they were married – four years ago – he had served six months in Wandsworth for a brutal assault on a complete stranger with whom a quarrel over some trivial matter had flared up during a drinking session in a pub.

The stranger had foolishly tried to take part in a private argument and Roger Tranter had turned on him savagely.

'I don't like people interfering in my affairs,' he explained later. 'If any silly bugger interferes with me he's in trouble.'

Mollie Dawson (as she was then) married her man as soon as he came out of prison. That he had served a term in gaol didn't worry her in the slightest; that he had a violent temper if he was roused put an edge on things; in some respects she liked violence in men. Tranter had twice knocked her about, and although she had screamed and fought back like a wild cat at the time, she didn't bear him any lasting malice over the episodes.

In the immediate post-Wandsworth days Tranter had a job driving a heavy lorry for a firm of contractors and was earning good money. He was acknowledged to be an exceptionally good driver, but, true to form, he managed to quarrel with most of his mates. 'If you don't get rid of that quarrelsome sod you won't have a man left on the site,' the foreman advised his boss.

The boss solved the problem by promoting Tranter to be his own private chauffeur, a position which he held for six months. At the end of that time the contractor found his firm bankrupted and bought out in one of Frederick Matton's large-scale financial jugglings and one result of the complicated affair was that Matton, who was looking for a new chauffeur at the time, acquired Roger Tranter.

The two men suited one another admirably. Matton wanted not only a good driver but somebody who could do a bit of strong-arm keeping-trespassers-at-bay work as well. He knew about his new chauffeur's record and he wasn't in the least concerned by it; a chauffeur had nothing whatever to do with the Videx books and that was the area in which Matton was vulnerable.

For his part Tranter frankly admired his new boss. 'Matton's a villain,' he told Mollie, 'like a lot of these big men in the City. They wouldn't be big men and in the big money if they weren't villains. They don't break into banks and get the stuff that way; it's cleverer than that, more civilised. They buy people up, squeeze them out of business, fix up transfers and take-overs and God knows what. And end up with the cash. Oodles of it. And good luck to them I say. I like villains: I understand them; I don't see how the world can go on without villainy; this gentle-Jesus, love-thy-neighbour guff is all right for the parsons but it doesn't get you anywhere. As long as Matton pays me good money I'll look after him.'

For the first few months of being in Lodge Cottage, Mollie saw very little of her husband's new employer; Matton was constantly on the Continent, mostly in Brussels and Paris, and was absent from Sweeting more often than he was there.

The pressure of Continental business eased somewhat and Matton began to be more regularly at Leys. One weekend, when an important American associate had to be entertained, everything was thrown into confusion because Mrs Watts, the Leys cook, went down suddenly with 'flu. As a last minute, last hope, expedient Mollie let herself be persuaded into filling the gap. She did so reluctantly because when Tranter had taken her to Lodge Cottage she had been emphatic about one thing – she was never going to be talked into doing domestic work at the big house.

'Just this once,' she said, 'and I mean it, just this one time, to help out.'

At the end of the evening Matton was feeling very well pleased with the world; the American had proved unexpectedly amenable and things looked rosy. Prompted by an unusual access of good nature he paid a visit to the kitchen to say thank you to the emergency cook.

For a few minutes they were alone in the kitchen; Matton was in good spirits and he had had a lot to drink.

Eventually he walked away from the kitchen thoughtfully. 'My God, I never knew Tranter had a wife like that,' he said to himself.

Two days later he called at Lodge Cottage.

'Roger's up in London; I sent him to the office with the car. I thought I'd call round to see how you were and to thank you again for the other night.'

The woman wasn't altogether surprised to see him there. She smiled slowly at him; and her first words were both an acknowledgement of what was going to happen and a warning about what would be a prime concern for both of them.

'People might see you coming here,' she said, 'and they'd know Roger was away.'

'That is precisely why I am not coming in,' Matton said. 'Do you know Silverman's Wood?'

'I've heard of it.'

'There's a hut on the edge of it. Used to be a shepherd's shelter, or some such thing. Nobody goes there these days – but we could; you could be blackberrying . . .'

Before her marriage to Tranter the woman had been fairly promiscuous. It was not an expression she would have used; in her mind it would have carried overtones of something wrong, it might even have suggested the archaic word 'sinful' to her; and, for her part, Mollie Dawson saw nothing wrong in what she was doing – she was so constructed that she wanted men, and if men were willing (and they often were) she took them.

When she became Mollie Tranter her appetite for men had not lessened, but she had had to walk warily; fear had kept her virtuous; the woman who was essentially a trollop had been an unerring wife for four years.

She was not a person given to analysing her feelings and she would have found it difficult to explain, even to herself, the strength of her reaction to the man whose mistress she had now become. For all her physical hunger she was also, in a curious way, fastidious; there were plenty of men she could not be bothered with, but in Frederick Matton she had found someone who affected her strongly. At their very first encounter, and increasingly since, something had flared up between them which neither of them bothered to explain but which both felt intensely.

Their first visit to the shepherd's hut was the precursor of many others; the woman was only too well aware of the danger of what she was doing; but she could not help doing it and, in a way, the danger added to the enjoyment.

Now, back from the Arms with her bottle of sherry, she looked round the living room of Lodge Cottage.

The tidiness of the place amused her. Since starting her affair with Frederick Matton she had found herself taking a good deal more trouble about running her home. She could not explain this, but it was quite noticeable, so much so that Roger Tranter had commented on it. 'Smartening things up a bit, aren't you?' he had said once and had, naturally, missed the point of his wife's laughter at the remark.

The sound of the front-door bell disturbed the woman's contemplation of the room. Callers at Lodge Cottage were not frequent and she wondered who it could be. It couldn't be Matton, she decided; too dangerous; yet as she moved towards the door she had an irrational half-hope that it might be.

When she opened the door the man she saw wasn't Matton; but it was someone she recognised. They had bumped into one another in the doorway of the Cobalt Arms. She could not imagine what had brought him to the cottage, so her greeting was a tentative, 'Yes?'

It had been easy enough for Aston to find out where Sir Frederick Matton's chauffeur lived; he made his way there hoping, at that time of day, to find the chauffeur's wife alone.

To go there was a foolish thing to do, but the truth was that the business of playing the part of a man of action had gone to Herbert Aston's head; he had a vague idea that by questioning the chauffeur's wife he might discover something which he could use against Matton. That what he was doing was taking him into highly dangerous waters didn't fully occur to him.

'Yes?'

'Is this where Mr Tranter lives?'

'It is; but I'm afraid Roger's not at home at the moment. He's out, working. Did you want to see him?'

'On the contrary, I wanted to see you.'

Mollie Tranter stared at the little man and smiled slightly. It wasn't possible, surely, that he had followed her to the cottage because of that brief, accidental meeting at the Cobalt Arms . . . ?

'You wanted to see me?' she asked. 'What about?'

'Do you know a place called Silverman's Wood?'

It was the very question which Matton had asked her at the beginning of their affair and it alarmed her. It alarmed her very much.

'I've heard of it,' she admitted after a pause.

'And there's a hut there, just beyond the wood.'

The woman's heart began to thump uncomfortably. 'A hut?' she parried. 'Is there? What of it?'

'I saw you come out of it yesterday afternoon.'

She knew now that she was in real danger; once or twice before in her life she had found herself in similar straits and instinct told her to take the bold way out.

'I've no idea what you are talking about,' she declared. 'Who are you, anyway? And what were you doing up in Silverman's Wood?'

'I started off on the public footpath, then I lost track of it and ended up at the edge of the wood near the hut.'

'And you say you saw me come out of this hut place?'

'That is precisely what I am saying,' Aston assured her in neat professional tones.

'You're making a mistake,' Mollie said. 'Yesterday? I never went near Silverman's Wood yesterday. You must have seen somebody else. Some other woman from the village. Lots of them go up there blackberrying.'

She was a very good liar and Aston looked hard at her, undecided for a moment. Then he shook his head and smiled. 'No, no,' he said, 'I know it was you. I'm sure I'm not mistaken. If I may say so, you have somewhat remarkable looks.'

'Are you trying something on? Bumping into me as I was going into the pub and then following me here and talking about my looks?'

Herbert Aston was shocked. 'No, no,' he protested, 'nothing like that, of course not.'

'That's what it looks like to me. It looks very much like it. And what about this hut that I'm supposed to have come out of? Did you see anybody else come out of it?'

'If you weren't there, that wouldn't be of any interest to you, would it?'

'What's of interest to me,' Mollie declared, 'is that I don't want lies told about me in the village. I don't know what your game is but you want to be careful. You may have seen somebody come out of the hut but it wasn't me. It was somebody else. I wasn't there.' She shut the door and left Aston on the step uncertain what to do next. In the living room of

Lodge Cottage, Mollie steadied herself with her arm on the back of a chair. She was trembling. *Christ Almighty,* she thought, *I knew something like this would happen. It was bound to in time. This is dangerous. I've got to play this very carefully indeed . . .*

Her thoughts went very quickly . . . probably best not to say anything to Roger; keep my trap shut . . . with a bit of luck this stranger staying at the Arms will have gone in a couple of days and nothing will come of it . . .

This tentative decision was blown sky high only a few moments after it was made by Roger Tranter's unexpectedly early return. From fifty yards down the village street he had seen Aston walking away from the cottage.

'Who was that at the door?' he asked. 'One of the Bible-pushing lot?'

His wife laughed easily, although her mouth was dry with fright (*Thank God you didn't come two minutes earlier, she thought*).

'Just about as barmy,' she said. 'He was up in the woods yesterday when I was blackberrying. He'd been on the path and lost it and wanted to know the way back to the village.'

'And what has he turned up here for, then?'

'He wants to do a bit of blackberrying himself and could I tell him the best places to go.'

Tranter stared at his wife reflectively. 'Sounds to me as though he's trying something on,' he said at last, 'as though he's trying to get fresh.'

Mollie laughed. 'Could be. One way and another most men seem to be at it most of the time. You ought to know all about that. But this one's harmless; no need to worry about him; just forget him. How come you're home so soon?'

'Matton doesn't want me this afternoon so I'm taking a bit of time off.'

'I dare say we'll find something to do.'

Tranter grinned. 'Suits me,' he said.

CHAPTER SIX

As good as a wink . . .

In the London office of Videx, Matton pressed the switch of the intercom on his desk.

'Mr Donaldson is coming in to see me in a moment,' he said. 'I don't want to be interrupted while he is in here. No phone calls; nothing.'

'Very good, Sir Frederick.'

While he was waiting for his accountant to arrive Matton walked across to the window and looked down on the grotesquely foreshortened view of the London street below him. He wasn't altogether happy about consulting Donaldson but the man had expert knowledge which had to be tapped; a grim little smile played across his face for a moment as he carried the thought out to its conclusion – tapped whilst he's still around . . .

The door opened and Matton turned sharply from the window; he hadn't heard a knock, but he didn't comment on the fact.

'Ah, come in, Donaldson,' he said.

The two men sat opposite one another, the huge flat-topped executive desk between them. Matton opened a cigarette box and pushed it across; the other man shook his head.

'Sorry to bother you,' Matton said. 'I expect you've plenty on your plate, as usual.'

'I was coming in to see you in any case.'

'Oh, were you? Well, let's get what I want to talk about out of the way first, shall we?'

'What is it?'

Matton took his time over lighting the cigarette he had chosen for himself; he was thinking, He won't be asking questions quite as rudely as that in a few months' time; he won't be asking any questions at all; he'll be out on his ear; aloud he said:

'It goes back quite a time, back to the time, in fact, when we took over Oxtone.'

The accountant was surprised. The Oxtone take-over lay in the past. Dead and buried. And in his opinion would be much better left that way.

'I hadn't joined the firm then,' he said.

'But you knew all about the take-over, all the details of it.'

Donaldson smiled slightly. 'Very much so,' he said, 'but what's the point in going into all that again? What's the percentage in bringing that up now?'

Matton answered irritably. 'I haven't the slightest wish to bring it up; but something has happened which may make it necessary for me to have all the facts and figures at my finger-tips. If one of those damned journalists in the Sunday press started to dig up a story about it things might be very awkward. And then these interviews on the box. They've got you by the short hairs. If you refuse to be interviewed you're guilty, everybody believes that. If you let yourself be interviewed, you don't stand a chance. The smart alec asking the questions is used to it all – the lights, the cameras, the studio, everything. You don't know what the hell it's all about and in any case he's asking the wrong questions, loaded questions; then by the time you're beginning to get into your stride and get an answer or two together the bastard says, "Sorry, I'm afraid that's all we have time for now," and you're switched off.'

'Is anybody wanting to interview you about the Oxtone takeover, then?'

'Not yet, no. And in all probability nobody will. But I believe in being ready for things. As I say, I want all the facts and figures at my finger-tips, not that I have slightest intention of giving the public all the facts and figures.'

'I should hope not,' Donaldson said a little grimly.

'But in order to know what not to say,' Matton went on, 'you've got to have the whole picture in your mind, so I want a précis, from the financial and company law angle, of everything that happened when we took over Oxtone. All right?'

The accountant didn't say whether it was all right or not. He was astonished by the Oxtone affair rising up out of the past like this; astonished and curious.

'You said something has happened to make all this necessary,' he said.

Matton nodded.

'What is it?'

Again the blunt question, rudely put. Matton decided to ignore the bluntness and rudeness for the present. For the present it was desirable to keep the accountant in a good temper – for the present.

'You remember Notas, the thing we developed into our Threedy?'

Yes, Donaldson remembered Notas.

'Did you ever realise what Notas was? I don't mean the thing itself but the word.'

'The word?'

'It's an anagram of Aston, the name of the man who had the original idea.'

'Edward Aston, wasn't it?'

'That's right. He died, of course, a long time ago. But now a brother of his has turned up. Apparently Edward Aston's daughter committed suicide the other day. This brother heard the news and went round to see the widow; he has taken no notice of her for twenty-eight years, mind you, and now he has suddenly come to the conclusion that her husband – Edward Aston – was hard done by at the take-over and that we owe him, now *her*, a lot of money.'

'After twenty-eight years?' Donaldson shook his head.

'Agreed. But if this brother takes it into his head to approach one of the City editors in Fleet Street and suggest that he starts to run a detailed story about the take-over – we don't want that, do we?'

'I should think it's the last thing you would want.'

You, not *we*, Matton noticed.

'You've seen this brother?'

'He came to see me. At Leys. He's putting up at the local pub, the Cobalt Arms.'

'What sort is he?'

'The clever sort. Finicky. Woolly-headed. Bleating on about justice and so on. Probably one of these bloody Socialists – *what wicked stuff this money is that you've got such a lot of, give me some of it at once.*'

'Sounds a bit of a crank to me. Why don't you just send him packing?'

'He'll be sent packing all right, don't bother. But in case he turns nasty and tries any tricks I want to be prepared, that's why I want that précis. O.K.?'

'You can have a précis if you want it,' Donaldson said.

'I do want it; that's what I called you in for, to tell you I wanted it.'

'I don't think I've told you how I got on in Paris, have I?'

'I never knew why you felt you had to go to Paris in the first place; it wasn't necessary.'

'I found it interesting though.'

'Was it?' Matton smiled sardonically. 'Personally I can do without all these committee meetings and conferences. You know what a conference is? A lot of people you call together when you haven't got the guts to make up your own mind. What was so interesting about this one?'

'The American was there – what's his name? Delabanque, isn't it?'

'I don't know why the Paris lot ever put him on the payroll.'

'Apparently he's not going to be on it for long.'

Matton looked up sharply; he had sensed something unusual about the other man's behaviour all through the interview; now instinct told him that he was coming near the explanation of it. He said nothing and waited.

'He's resigning; he's sending his letter in right away,' Donaldson added.

Matton smiled; he felt relieved; if Delabanque went of his own accord it was one possible trouble out of the way. But the next sentence jolted him.

'It will save you the trouble of sacking him, anyway.'

'Who says I was thinking of sacking him?'

'I do. Just as you intend to sack me and God knows how many other people as well. Half the firm apparently.'

Matton stretched across for the cigarettes, picked one out and lit it deliberately. He was thinking hard. For a second or two he toyed with the idea of denying everything, but he decided that this was an occasion when the technique of the plain, straightforward lie wouldn't serve. Obviously there had been a leak and that was a matter that would have to be looked into; for the moment he had an awkward situation on his hands.

'Well, you won't have the pleasure of sacking me,' Donaldson went on, 'because I am going to do exactly the same as Delabanque. You'll be getting my resignation in writing this evening.'

'Do you mean to say that you are walking out and leaving the firm at a few hours' notice just like that?'

'Exactly like that. This is the last day I'm going to work here.'

'You're breaking your contract.'

'Are you going to try to do anything about it? Are you really going to run the risk of my getting up in court and telling people a few, just a few, of the things I know about this firm?'

Matton stared at the accountant long and hard. At length he said, 'I never did much care for you, Donaldson.'

Donaldson laughed and answered, 'You didn't? I'm glad to hear it; and, in common with a number of other people on the staff, I have long been of the opinion, Matton, that you are a prize bastard and I'm delighted to be able to tell you so at last.' He got up out of his chair and walked towards the door.

The head of Videx watched him go and at the very last moment bawled out, '*Donaldson*.'

The accountant turned, the door already half open. When Matton spoke again his voice was ugly with venom. 'All right,' he said, 'walk out on me. Don't do another hour's work.

Shut your books up and go. Only just remember this – I'll fix things so that you'll never get another decent job anywhere in this city, or anywhere else if I can do anything about it. You think I'm a prize bastard; by God I'll act like one. I'll smash you, Donaldson; now get out.'

Herbert Aston sat in his bedroom at the Cobalt Arms reading. His chair was tilted back at a comfortable angle, his slippered feet rested on the edge of the bed. Whenever he went away from home his habit was to take two books with him, one that mattered and one that didn't; or, as he sometimes described it, a meal and a snack. For the Sweeting visit the meal was a selection of Tennyson's poems, the snack an entertaining light-weight paperback which he had already disposed of by lending it to a bookless Hooky Hefferman.

Aston was feasting on *Locksley Hall*; the very description of its metre delighted him – *truncated trochaic octometers* – he wondered if his admirable pupil Dorothea knew the technical words and if she took as much pleasure from them as he did; it struck him as a possible subject for an essay – *Discuss (with examples) what proportion of the pleasure which we derive from a word is due to its sound alone and how much to the association of its meaning*.

Presently, having had enough of *Locksley Hall* for the time being, he slipped Tennyson into his pocket and decided to go downstairs. When he reached the hall Mrs Old was not at the desk but a man had just come in from the street.

The newcomer, seeing someone who was obviously staying in the place, asked, 'Are you Mr Aston?'

The Professor was so much enjoying the game of being somebody else that he was positively startled to hear his real name.

'What if I am?' he parried.

'The brother of the late Edward Aston?'

'I'm afraid I don't know who you are – ' Aston said uncertainly.

'My name is Donaldson. I'm – I *was* – the chief accountant

in a firm called Videx. Is there some place where we could talk?'

'We could go into the coffee room,' Aston suggested. 'I don't suppose there'll be anybody there.'

There wasn't anybody in the coffee room; it was small, square in shape and a little cheerless. Donaldson studied the man he had run to earth and didn't quite know what to make of him. Like most men whose lives are bounded by money and big business, the accountant was a poor judge of character outside those inhibiting limits. He drew a packet of cigarettes from his pocket and extended it.

'Cigarette?'

Aston shook his head.

'Mind if I do?'

'Not in the slightest. I don't like cigarettes but I'm in favour of other people smoking them; it cuts down the population and helps pay the taxes. Please smoke.'

The accountant's smile was a trifle forced; just like Matton said, he thought, one of the clever sort. One of the *nonners*: no cigarettes, probably no drinks, and very likely a vegetarian into the bargain.

'I presume Sir Frederick Matton has sent you to see me,' Aston said.

Donaldson shook his head. 'On the contrary. Matton doesn't know I'm here. I've left Videx. I'm self-employed now – well, *un*employed at the moment.'

Aston was silent for some seconds while he turned this over in his mind. Along with his dislikes of tycoons went an almost pathological distrust of accountants; the Professor had only the haziest idea of what an accountant did, but he was convinced that they were almost the chief sinners in the general villainy of big business. He wondered how much of what he was being told was true.

'How do you come to be interested in my brother?' he asked.

'I understand that you think Videx – which really means Matton – treated your brother badly?'

'My brother was swindled out of a fortune; but that is the

way big-business men go on, isn't it? You ought to know that being an accountant. In my view business tycoons are parasites on society, and accountants, and their like, are parasites on the tycoons.'

'I wonder if we could leave out your political views for a moment?'

The Professor laughed. He was enjoying himself. As soon as you got one of these high-powered business men into an argument, he thought, they don't stand a chance. Logic bowls 'em over like ninepins.

'No, you can't,' he answered. 'I don't know how much Greek you remember. *Polis* a city, or state. By extension the business of running a state, the whole apparatus of government and, ultimately, of living together in society. How can you discuss anything outside that framework?'

'Mr Aston, I didn't come here to talk politics.'

'I'm trying to point out to you that in a sense it's hardly possible to talk anything else. In your terms what *did* you come here to talk about?'

'I understand that certain circumstances recently caused you to get in touch with your late brother's widow.'

It was clear now to the Professor that Matton and this henchman of his had been discussing him together; he was convinced that Matton had sent the Videx accountant, full of lies and guile, to spy out the land. Well, he won't get very far, Aston thought, not against me.

'When you say *certain circumstances*,' he said, 'I presume you are referring to the fact that my brother's daughter committed suicide?'

'I'm sorry to hear about that.'

'Are you? Why? You never knew the girl.'

Donaldson, who was easily at home amid a bewildering mass of figures and statistics, felt out of his depth. How the hell do you tackle a prickly customer like this, he thought. Inhuman, talking about a suicide like that . . .

Making his tone of voice as reasonable as he could he said, 'I was wondering if when you talked with your sister-in-law she showed you any specific document, or agreement, or letter – any undertaking of any sort between Videx and your late brother?'

'If she had done I wouldn't show it to you.'

'Look, Mr Aston, you've got me all wrong. We're on the same side.'

'I sincerely hope not,' the Professor replied tartly. 'If I knew of any such document I should confront Matton with it; as it is I can only rely on trying to shame him into a sense of justice.'

Donaldson began to realise that he was wasting his time trying to get anything out of this sharp-tongued little know-all. The idea of shaming the head of Videx into a sense of justice amused him; in his experience not many fortunes had been made in the City by a strict adherence to a sense of justice.

He laughed. 'O.K.,' he said, 'have it your own way. But in my opinion you'll be lucky if you shame Matton into anything.'

'For the first time since you started talking I'm inclined to agree with you,' Aston replied. 'A man who will seduce his chauffeur's wife is probably past shame.'

Donaldson, who had already half risen from his seat preparatory to leaving, sat down again slowly and looked hard at the other man. Just general venom, or was there any substance to it? he wondered . . .

'If you take my advice – ' he said.

'I won't,' Aston cut in happily. 'I don't take advice from other people, especially people like you.'

The accountant flushed a little but went on quietly enough, 'It's highly dangerous making libellous statements like that; you can get yourself into a lot of trouble.'

'A moment ago you were trying to convince me that we were on the same side. Now you are threatening me; I suppose Matton sent you here for that very purpose. The trouble with you people is that you are so stupidly imprecise. I didn't make a libellous statement about anybody; I merely enunciated what I consider to be a general truth – that a man who has an affair with the wife of his chauffeur is probably past feeling shame about most things; just as I make the general observation that if I am bird-watching in the woodlands and I see a woman come out of a hut, followed a few minutes later by a man, I am entitled to my own opinion as to why they went in there, and please don't imagine for one moment that any threats from you will make me change that opinion.'

'I'm quite sure they wouldn't,' Donaldson said; he stubbed out his cigarette, rose to his feet and left the coffee room.

When Mollie Tranter came to the door of Lodge Cottage and saw the firm's accountant standing there, although she was not expecting him she was not particularly surprised. She didn't know (no outsiders yet knew) anything about Donaldson's resignation and she assumed that he had come, as he occasionally had done in the past, with orders for her husband.

Donaldson had been banking on the likelihood that the chauffeur would not be at home and on the way to the cottage he had thought up a story to explain his visit.

'Is Roger in?' he asked.

'I'm afraid not, Mr Donaldson. Has Sir Frederick sent you with any orders for him?'

Donaldson hadn't taken much notice of the chauffeur's wife before; now he studied her with interest; what he saw intrigued him; just Matton's type, he thought, maybe there's something in it after all . . .

'No, it isn't that,' he said, 'I was hoping Roger could give me a bit of help. I've got my car in the village and for the moment I'm stuck there. I can't get a spark out of the damned thing. I was going to ask Roger to have a look at it for me.'

'Of course he would if he was here, Mr Donaldson. I don't think he's far; he might even be in the Arms, having his pint.'

'I've just come from the Arms.'

'And Roger wasn't there?'

'No, the only chap there is an odd sort of cove babbling on about being up in the woods and a hut up there. Some tale or other about it. Well, if Roger isn't in he can't help me, can he?'

'No. I'm sorry about that,' Mollie Tranter said in a subdued voice.

Donaldson walked away from Lodge Cottage well pleased with his little ploy. When he had spoken about the woods and the hut he had been watching the woman's face intently. Without any question something had shown itself in her eyes. Alarm and fear. She had been touched in a sensitive spot and she had shown it. The accountant went along the road slowly, wondering just exactly what it was that he had stumbled upon and just exactly how he could make the most use of it.

In the village he encountered the chauffeur who was on his way home.

'I've just been to your place, Roger.'

'Oh, sorry I wasn't there, Mr Donaldson. Any change in the orders for tomorrow?'

'Not that I know of. What's happening tomorrow?'

'I've got to be at Reading all day to run the E.E.C. people about.'

'Is Sir Frederick going?'

'No; all the E.E.C. lot want is a taxi really, and I'm taking the Mercedes there to supply it. Nice work if you can get it, isn't it?'

Donaldson laughed. 'Nothing to do with me what the outside people get up to,' he said. 'I've come to ask you to have a look at my car. I can't get it to start.'

'Where is it?'

'Outside the Arms.'

'Well, we'll have to see what can be done, won't we?'

When they reached the stationary Rover the chauffeur asked for the keys, sat in the driving seat and switched on.

The engine obediently came to life at once.

Donaldson feigned surprise and delight. 'Well, I don't know,' he said. 'I couldn't get a squeak out of it. What do you suppose it was?'

Tranter switched off and climbed out of the car. He shrugged his shoulders.

'God knows. She sounds O.K. now, though. She's running sweet enough.'

'Thanks a lot, Roger. Sorry to have troubled you. Incidentally, I shan't be troubling you much in the future.'

'How's that, then?'

'I'm leaving the firm – have left it, in fact.'

'You've left Videx, Mr Donaldson?'

Donaldson nodded.

'What on earth has made you do that?'

'Matton and I have fallen out about one or two things. I don't mean financial things in the firm, but the way he behaves outside. Women and so on. Other men's wives. Still, I expect you know as much about all that as I do.'

The chauffeur stared hard at the other man and said nothing.

Donaldson laughed. 'Well, there you are,' he said. 'They say a nod's as good as a wink to a blind horse. Thanks a lot for fixing the car. I've got to be going.'

Roger Tranter watched the car thoughtfully as it moved away down the village street.

CHAPTER SEVEN

After bigger game

Almost directly outside the Arms, Herbert Aston was cannoned into by a boy who, skateboard out of control, arms and legs flying, ended up in a heap against one of the few lamp-posts in the village.

'What's going on then?' P.C. West enquired. The question struck the Professor's logical mind as being singularly asinine; in his opinion what was going on was perfectly evident. The boy got to his feet grinning a trifle nervously: in common with all the other village boys he knew P.C. West only too well.

'I'm O.K.,' he announced. 'I'm not hurt.'

'More's the pity,' said the policeman, bending down and picking up the skateboard. 'Dangerous things these.'

'Not half as dangerous as you on your motor-cycle,' young Charlie Dent answered. 'Can I have my skateboard back?'

P.C. West ignored this request and turned to Aston whom he recognised as the stranger staying at the Arms. 'You all right?' he enquired.

'I am perfectly all right,' Aston answered crisply. 'The boy didn't hurt me in any way at all.'

'You're lucky then. These skateboards will be the death of somebody before long. They ought to be banned.'

'The mere fact that a thing is a possible cause of death is hardly sufficient reason for banning it,' Aston said in his best tutorial manner. 'If it were, most things in life would be banned – but perhaps that would please you, officer?'

One of the clever, clever sort, West thought. *Officer* this and *officer* that. Don't you dare to step one inch out of line, officer, in the performance of your duty, but be sure you come running double quick, officer, if ever I get into trouble myself and dial 999 . . .

'Can I have my skateboard back?' Charlie Dent reiterated.

'No, you can't.'

'As a matter of interest,' Aston enquired, 'why can't the boy have his property back?'

'As a matter of interest, because I consider it dangerous.'

Aston turned to the boy. 'What do you call this contraption of yours, boy? A skateboard, is it?'

'Of course it's a skateboard,' Charlie answered. 'Everybody knows that.'

'Marvellous what everybody knows and what everybody doesn't know,' P.C. West said, 'and how some people will come poking their fingers into things as don't concern them in the slightest.'

'To see justice done is the duty of every citizen,' the Professor announced rather pompously.

'Don't start talking to me about citizen's duty,' the policeman answered sharply. 'I'll believe in citizens doing their duty when I see it happening. If I'm trying to arrest a violent drunk and getting the worst of it I don't see you wading in to help. You'll be like the rest of them, cross the road and hurry off home to write a letter to the paper saying isn't the violence in the streets awful. A citizen's duty, that you sound so keen about, is to back us chaps up when we are trying to prevent an illegal act.'

'Are these skateboard things illegal?' Aston enquired.

'No they aren't,' Charlie Dent cut in, 'that's why I want mine back.'

'You can have your skateboard back, young Dent, if you come to the station for it this afternoon; when you do the Sergeant will read you a lesson about being a bloody nuisance,' the law told him.

Recognising the futility of battling against superior force, Charlie Dent slunk away muttering his angry discontent.

The Professor was beginning to enjoy himself; hitherto any participation in public affairs which he had felt disposed to make had been confined to writing a letter to *The Times* (usually unprinted); he was finding the present confrontation much more fun.

'In my opinion – ' he led off, only to be cut short by the law which said in its unattractive voice which had a flat Midland twang about it, 'I'm not interested in your opinion. When I want to know your opinion I'll ask for it, and then I most likely won't take it.'

Recognising a re-statement of his own view on such matters Aston was obliged to laugh.

'I'm bound to say I rather agree with you there,' he said. 'You've said something sensible for a change; but it still seems to me that you are acting in a high-handed and indefensible manner.'

'Does it?' P.C. West enquired. 'Well, it seems to me that you are acting like an interfering busybody, and you're coming damned near to obstructing me in the performance of my duty.'

The Professor made a gesture of stopping his ears. 'I do beg of you,' he said, 'not to take refuge in officialese; please don't insult my intelligence by a bombardment of verbal clichés, and please don't add foolishness to your tyrannical behaviour.'

'I haven't insulted anybody,' the policeman retorted. 'And what are you accusing me of now? What foolishness?'

'I am accusing you of forgetting that you are a public servant, your wages paid by the ratepayers, and of acting *ultra vires*.'

'P'raps if you well-off ratepayers dished out a little more in the way of wages you'd get a better service. What's all this got to do with you, anyway? You're just poking your nose in. You're just doing a bit of police-bashing for fun. Everybody else does it and gets away with it so why shouldn't you? If you aren't careful I shall be asking you to come down to the station as well.'

'I should be delighted to do so,' Aston averred, 'and I should take the opportunity of impressing on the Sergeant the desirability of teaching his underlings elementary good manners.'

Hooky Hefferman had come on the scene in time to hear the last exchanges. Without knowing what the *casus* was he realised that something like *belli* was going on, and that it might be wise to extricate his fellow resident at the Arms from the imbroglio. A long time ago the Chinese philosopher Chi-Lung wrote: *When the dark clouds of tragedy threaten thunder the wise man seeks to lighten matters by the judicious introduction of a farcical fart.* Recalling this earthy but admirable piece of advice, Hooky intervened in his best imitation of Dock Green behaviour.

' 'Allo, 'allo, 'allo. What's all this 'ere?'

P.C. West was apparently not on the Dock Green wavelength. 'And you keep out of it, too,' he advised threateningly. 'I don't want any of your Private Eye pantomime around here. You don't seem to have anything better to do than drink in the bar of the Arms, so I suggest you do just that and leave me to get on carrying out my duties.'

Herbert Aston watched him go away down the village street. 'An interesting encounter,' was his verdict. 'I find myself enlarging my experiences considerably. I think I shall write a letter to *The Times* drawing attention to the lamentable decay of manners in the police force.'

Hooky laughed; he occasionally cast an eye over the Printing House Square postbag: as he said, a man has to find some way to keep himself amused in these dull days. In his opinion the early-cuckoo merchants, the longevity recorders, and the 'it was not F. J. C. Peters who played for Surrey in 1906 but his cousin F.P.G.' experts would welcome the advent of the Sweeting bird-watcher.

'You do that,' he said. 'You write to Auntie Times. Just your cup of tea.'

'The constable actually confiscated from one of the village boys a thing called a skateboard the boy was using.'

'Damned good idea,' Hooky said. 'Skateboards are bloody dangerous.'

'I was concerned about the boy's rights.'

'You're wasting your time. Boys haven't got any rights. If what goes on continually inside the mind of a boy of fourteen was made public the lad would be sent to Borstal at once.'

'All the same, on general principles I don't care to see authority abused.'

'You must have a thin time then, chum, looking round the world.'

'I haven't been much in the habit of looking round it hitherto,' the Professor said, 'and I must confess that I am rather enjoying doing so.'

'Still, give him his due, the fuzz did make one sensible remark.'

'The fuzz?'

'The law; the underpaid, unregarded prop of your comfort and mine. The man who takes the road shocks whilst we ride in the cushioned back seat of the car. The man we cheerfully give devilish jobs to and then expect him to act like an angel, in this case P.C. Sardonic West.'

'You say he made one sensible remark?'

'He did, indeed. He may have made many more, I only came up at the tail-end of your interesting little tête-à-tête; but he was definitely on target with one thing he said, so let's go inside and put it into practice.'

The rotund and rubicund Old was behind the bar polishing glasses.

'Your usual Pimms is it, Mr Hefferman?' he enquired.

'And a small dry Sercial for my ornithological friend,' Hooky ordered, adding, 'And that's a word I shan't be using much if I stay here any length of time.'

The Professor was pleased with the word. 'I'm glad to see you remember your Greek roots,' he said. 'Ornis a bird. So many young people who come up to the University these days have no regard whatsoever for the classics. As for the matter of refreshment, I think I'll extend my experience a little further and try one of the things you are drinking – a Pimms, do you call it?'

'A marvellous shield and buckler against the onslaught of Fate,' Hooky assured him.

Herbert Aston watched the preparation of his Pimms with the interest of a child observing some new sort of experiment. He sipped the finished product with the attentive appreciation of a connoisseur and in the end gave it his qualified approval. 'It gives me a gratifying sense of well-being,' was his verdict, 'possibly illusory but agreeable nevertheless, rather like religion.'

'Try another,' Hooky suggested. 'No good trying to fly on one wing.'

But the Professor was not to be persuaded to venture into the biplane world; he had caught sight of the clock behind the bar.

'I must be going,' he said, 'I've something to do.'

'Chasing the crested corn creepers again?' Hooky asked.

Herbert Aston smiled. 'I'm after rather bigger game than birds,' he said.

'What do you suppose our little nature fancier meant by that?' Hooky asked when he and the innkeeper were left alone.

Old laughed and said, 'I never worry about what people say, Mr Hefferman. It wouldn't do in this job. People say a lot of funny things when you come to add it up.'

'By God, you're right there,' Hooky agreed. 'A hell of a lot of mysterious things go on inside everybody's head, that's what makes it all so interesting.'

When he was halfway up the drive to Leys, Aston was confronted by Roger Tranter who was astonished to see him there. Like most men of violence the chauffeur was suspicious; he had not been entirely satisfied by Mollie's account of the stranger's visit to Lodge Cottage and now the sight of him on his way to the big house started all sorts of doubts and wonderings.

'What are you wanting here?' he asked.

'I'm on my way to see Frederick Matton.'

'*Sir* Frederick to you. What do you want to see him about?'

Completely unalarmed by the aggressive tone of the question, Aston answered, 'I rather think that is my concern.'

'You've come to make a bloody nuisance of yourself, just like you did at my cottage with all this blackberrying business.'

'Blackberrying business?'

'You said you wanted to know the best places to go blackberrying; that's what you told my wife, wasn't it?'

'Es is immer gut etwas zu wissen.'

'What the hell are you on about now? What's all that? A dirty crack or something?'

The Professor laughed. 'Goethe. Allow me to translate – it is always good to know something, or I suppose you could say *all knowledge is good*. If your wife can tell me the best local spots for blackberrying, and for other rural activities, I am always willing to learn. Now if you will kindly step to one side I will go and see Matton.'

Roger Tranter hesitated a moment, then he moved out of the way; he watched the stranger thoughtfully as he made his way to the house.

Inside Leys, Matton said, 'I'm usually in the London office at this time of day. You're lucky to find me in.'

'On the whole I think I'm a lucky person,' Aston replied blandly.

'You sound smug enough about it. As a matter of interest, what do you do? What's your job?'

'I am a university professor.'

'I might have guessed it. I suppose you're mixed up with all these damned students.'

'Very much so, and believe me I damn them often enough myself. By the way, where were you educated?'

'On top of London buses mostly. Out of books. I educated myself. And, incidentally, some bits of knowledge can be dangerous; you're a clever man, I'm sure you realise that.'

Aston nodded. 'Indeed I do,' he answered happily, 'and, of course, some bits of knowledge are valuable, aren't they?'

'So now we come down to the nitty-gritty.'

'It's an appalling expression,' the Professor said. 'It's an extraordinary thing in an age when the means of disseminating language have never been more widespread – newspapers, radio, television and so on – language itself, the essential thing they all exist to propagate, is contracting into a few withered clichés and rapidly dying.'

'Some other time.'

'I beg your pardon?'

'I don't want to listen to one of your university lectures. I'm not one of your bloody protesting students. Save your breath. I said nitty-gritty and I mean nitty-gritty. So do you. The money. That's what it's all about. That's what you've come for, isn't it?'

'I've never objected to a directness of approach, in fact it's a virtue that I try to instil in my pupils. So the answer to your question is *yes*, I have come for money; but it is *yes* with a qualification; what brought me here was a desire to see a wrong put right, a sense of justice.'

'God help us all.'

'If there is a God maybe he will; let us hope so, anyway; but I can't quite see the relevance of your remark.'

'Ever read any history?'

'It's not my subject.'

'Not mine either; but if I read anything it's always history. Modern history mostly. And do you know what history is? It's a catalogue of wars, nothing else. And there isn't a single war that's ever been waged which wasn't started, so we are told, in order to put a wrong right and out of a sense of justice. We shall not sheathe the sword and so on. The Somme in nineteen-sixteen and Stalingrad and Vietnam, they were all fought out of a sense of justice – according to the politicians, who didn't take part in them, of course.'

'I'm not a politician.'

'Neither am I. I'm a business man. So I go back to what I said a moment ago, the nitty-gritty, the money. You're here to get as much money out of me as you can, is that right?'

'Entirely.'

'And if I refuse to pay, you think that you came across

something in the woods the other day which you could use to make things very awkward for me. Is that right as well?'

'I admire your grasp of the situation.'

'So on the whole it will be safer for me to pay up, eh?'

'It probably will.'

'Right. I'm going to pay up. I'm paying up partly because I want to get rid of you, and, although you may not believe it, partly because of what you told me about Edward Aston dying of T.B. and his widow being badly off and the girl committing suicide. Don't think I've gone all soft and sentimental. I haven't. I just want the simplest, quickest way out of the whole thing.'

Matton bent down, unlocked the bottom drawer in his desk and drew out a parcel. He put the parcel on the table.

'Ever seen a one-hundred-pound note?' he asked.

'I don't know that I have.'

Matton untied the parcel. 'There are fifty of them here,' he said. 'Five thousand quid, and never mind about inflation and all the rest of it, five thousand pounds is a lot of money. I know you asked for fifty thousand. Forget it. You're out of your depth. If you've got any sense you'll get back quickly to where you belong – the cloud-cuckoo-land of your university, nice and safe and unreal. You had better count the money; I'm only a business man, I might be trying to cheat you.'

Somewhat uncertainly Aston began to count the one-hundred-pound notes, fascinated by the sight of so many of them.

Matton watched and he seemed to find the sight mildly amusing. 'O.K.?' he asked finally.

'There are fifty notes there, yes; but – '

Matton interrupted with a gesture of his hand. 'Some little time ago you said you reckoned yourself to be a lucky person. I wonder if you realise how lucky. Suppose somebody overheard our conversation?'

'I never waste time on fruitless suppositions.'

'Smart alec, aren't you? Smart and smug like all you intellectual lot.'

A sheet of paper was lying on the table. Matton moved it to one side and picked up what was disclosed. Now he was patently amused.

'Know what that is?' he asked.

Aston did happen to know; he had seen a number of such things at the University. 'It's a tape-recorder,' he answered slowly.

'Quite right, a tape-recorder. So it wasn't such a fruitless supposition after all, was it? It's all there. Nice and clear and identifiable. Good evidence in a court of law. Do you happen to know anything about the law, clever Mister University Professor? I very much doubt it. I don't think you know much about anything. You've been reading fairy stories; you're trying to play Jack the Giant killer. Well, I do know quite a lot about the law. And I can tell you one thing for certain – the law doesn't like blackmail. Why, these days it's quite possible to kill somebody and get away with a suspended sentence, but there isn't a judge on the bench who'll give you a suspended sentence for blackmail. Blackmailers get put away for three, five, possibly even seven years.'

Suddenly Herbert Aston felt a lot less confident. 'Blackmail – ' he began uncertainly.

'Yes, blackmail. Don't tell me you didn't use the word. Of course you didn't use it. And the law doesn't require you to. Demanding money by menaces, that's what the law calls it. And that's precisely what you did.' Matton tapped the tape-recorder. 'It's all here. Every word you uttered. And, believe me, when prosecuting Counsel gets hold of it in court you won't stand a chance. Not that there's any need for it to get to court, is there?'

'The decision seems to be in your hands.'

Matton laughed. 'That's just about the first really sensible thing I've heard you say,' he said. 'You're quite right, it is in my hands. O.K., let's have a look at things – what's the position? We've each scored a goal and the whistle's gone. That's the way I see it. So like reasonable people we agree to call it a draw and pack up. You think you know something that could make things awkward for me. Maybe you do.' He held up the tape-recorder. 'I *know* I've got something here that can ruin your life – have you any idea what three years inside would do to you? And what price your university job when you came out? So it's tit for tat, isn't it? Stalemate. But you aren't going away empty-handed. Five thousand pounds is useful money, don't make any mistake about that. So take it; and, by God, you really can call yourself lucky.

'There's one condition, though; that you clear off, away, out of this village. Where's your car? At the Arms?'

'I haven't got a car. I regard the motor-car as anti-social.'

'You would! God Almighty, the amount of cock you clever fools talk. How did you get here?'

'By bus.'

'You'll have to go by bus then. And that means tomorrow. But it's got to be tomorrow. Go away and stay away. If ever I see you in these parts again, or if I hear from you in any way, I'll take this little fellow,' he tapped the tape-recorder, 'straight to the police and I'll hit you as hard as I can.'

CHAPTER EIGHT

87—9—0

Being a fundamentally sensible person (i.e. realising that when faced with any practical problem of daily living the best thing a man can do is to take it to a woman for its solution) Hooky had consulted Mrs Old over the matter of his blister. Martha Old was evidently delighted to have her opinion sought. 'A blister?' she said. 'Oh dear; never mind, I'm sure we can soon put that right.'

Masculine-wise Hooky felt that there was something vaguely ludicrous about a blister and that he ought to apologise for it.

'It's not a thing I normally have,' he explained, adding in self-laudatory extenuation, 'but then, I don't normally walk a hundred and fifty miles in seven days.'

Martha Old was not particularly impressed. 'Walking never hurt anyone, Mr Hefferman,' she said. 'When my mother was a girl she walked three miles to school every day and three miles back. This was when she was five, mind you; and she went on to be ninety-five.'

'Good for the old lady,' Hooky said, 'but I don't want to go on to ninety-five.'

'Not now you don't; but you wait till you're ninety-four. While there's life there's hope, as they say. Now then, about this blister of yours. I've got a sovereign cure for anything of that sort, I'll rummage it out.'

When the sovereign cure had been 'rummaged out' from a store cupboard full of homely treasures it was seen to be contained in a small earthenware pot of unusual, even sinister, shape. The pot being opened disclosed a dark-looking paste which smelt abominably.

'That's goose balm, that is,' Hooky was informed.

'Goose balm!' he cried in mock alarm. 'God Almighty, what next?'

'Ah, you can laugh, Mr Hefferman; but there's a lot of the old ways better than the new. The old world was a real one; things lasted. Now it's all three-ply and plastic. You can't buy goose balm in your supermarket. They wouldn't know what you were talking about. I learnt about it from my mother and she learnt from hers. That would be my grannie, and she was born in 1837. Sounds like before the Flood now, doesn't it? And when they wanted any more of it they had to go to the village wise woman, same as I did for mine.'

'A wise woman? A witch?'

'I didn't say witch, Mr Hefferman. I said wise woman.'

'And is there one in this village, now?'

Martha Old smiled. 'Don't you worry your head about that,' she advised. 'There's more things in life than a blind man sees, as they say. Now, then, this blister of yours – what you do is to rub a bit of the balm on with the thumb of your right hand. You've got to do it clockwise and you should say the words, only I won't tell you them because you'd laugh, and you'll find it won't worry you for long.'

Hooky did as he was bid. Using his right thumb and working in a clockwise direction he rubbed the evil-smelling dark paste over the offending blister.

When he woke up next morning there was no blister.

'It's gone; vanished,' he told Mrs Old. 'It's a miracle.'

She was amused at his exuberance. 'I don't know about miracle,' she said, 'but there's a lot of the old ways better than anything you can get today.'

Hooky, restored to comfortable mobility, declared his intention of staying on at the Arms for at least another day.

'I shall explore the village. I shall investigate rural England.'

'You do that, Mr Hefferman; you have a day out and this evening I'll have as nice a piece of cold roast beef waiting for you as you ever saw. With a baked potato. And there's still some of the Double Gloucester.'

'My God, Mrs Old,' Hooky declared reverently, 'you're a woman rooted in realities.'

It was an English sort of day, with plenty of blue sky, some wonderful white galleons of clouds and warmth in the sunshine in spite of a boisterous wind.

The village world of Sweeting lay open for discovery and Hooky, a metropolitan at heart, felt like Columbus as he set about discovering it.

Almost the first thing he saw was a large black Mercedes being driven off at speed. He recognised the car as the one which had unceremoniously splashed him with mud on the evening of his arrival, but this time he didn't see anybody in the back seat, the chauffeur appeared to be alone. The sight was of no particular interest to Hooky, who couldn't guess how keenly it was being observed by another pair of watching eyes.

Outside the Village Hall he studied the notice board. He was a great reader of *trivia*; no *War and Peace* merchant, Hooky Hefferman, he couldn't stay the course; too much like trying to eat your way through a flannel sandwich, he was wont to say; but odd scraps at the bottom of news columns; graffiti; torn bits of letters lying on the pavement, these jigsaw pieces he treasured like a magpie.

The Village Hall notice board offered typical fare. The W.I. met, it seemed, on Wednesday afternoons at three-thirty; there was to be a dance on the forthcoming Saturday; the A.G.M. of the Sweeting Cricket Club was scheduled for a fortnight ahead.

'Going to the dance, mister?'

Charlie Dent, skateboard in hand, stood at his side.

Hooky said no, he wouldn't be going to the dance.

'Neither am I. Girls are soppy.'

The verdict amused Hooky. He turned it over in his mind. It was not one which he could agree with. In a great deal of varied experience he had discovered girls to be slinky, kinky and winky; he was prepared to believe that they were wonderful, extraordinary, fascinating, queer; he had found them irresistible and unapproachable; they had proved themselves devastating and demanding, delightful and devilish; but *soppy*, no, he was not prepared to admit that.

'Are you a misogynist?' he enquired.

'Is that a rude word, mister? I collect rude words, I like them.'

'You should have a great future in the entertainment world,' Hooky assured him. 'I see you've got your skateboard back.'

'I went down to the station for it. They had to give it to me. Old Westy didn't want to, but it's my property; so in the end he had to; but he says if he catches me using it on the pavement he's going to give me a thick ear.'

On general principles the thick-ear approach to the young was one of which Hooky approved; but he was in an amiable mood so he contented himself by saying, 'If I were you, sonny, I'd try not to fall foul of the law. On the whole it doesn't pay.'

Charlie Dent was unimpressed by the advice. 'Fat-arse West doesn't know everything that goes on in the village, not by a long chalk,' he declared, and whistling with shrill discordancy, skateboard held firmly in hand, he walked jauntily away.

Moving on from the Village Hall, Hooky passed through the stir and bustle of a normal village morning; to his dismay he noted that what should have been an old-fashioned village shop facing the Green had been hideously transmogrified into a miniature supermarket; but to make up for this defection from the decencies the cricket ground – just beyond the Green – was splendidly authentic. The figures still hung on the board showing the final score in the last match of the season, 87—9—0; the hut which served as a pavilion was shuttered against the winter months and looked as unhappy as a theatre which is dark; the square in the middle of the field was decently roped off against marauding cattle. A wooden bench by the side of the pavilion was occupied by an ancient of days who, had he been transported to Hollywood, would have got a job on sight as the original, authentic dyed-in-the-wood rustic.

Whether this venerable figure had been sitting there ever since 87—9—0 went up on the board and would continue unmoving until the first ball of next season was bowled Hooky didn't know; but it seemed likely.

'You a cricketer?' the old man asked suspiciously.

Hooky, who had been in the eleven at Eton and had subsequently turned out occasionally for I Zingari, made the Englishman's answer:

'Here and there; bits and pieces.'

The ancient grunted. Bits and pieces didn't interest him, he remembered the high noon of the thing, the heroic days.

'I saw Gilbert Jessop play on this ground,' he said, 'nineteen hundred and five. Long before you were born. They were getting up money to pay for a new stand on the County ground and this was a charity match to help the funds. Gilbert Jessop's eleven against a local fifteen. People came from miles. Brakes, wagonettes, dog-carts, private carriages, all round the ground; you've never seen such a turn-out. Everyone desperate keen to see the Slogger make a hundred. I was only a lad then, putting the figures up on the board. They were supposed to toss up for who batted first. But Jessop wasn't having anything of that. He might have lost. Billy Green the blacksmith was captain of Sweeting at that time. 'No tossing, Green,' Jessop told him, 'these people have come to see me bat and in case it comes on to rain my side will go in first.' That's how cricket was run in those days; it was gentlemen and players then, remember; now there aren't any gentlemen left and the bloody players have all got accountants to deal with their super-tax.'

'So Jessop's side batted first, eh?'

'Like he said.'

'And when did he himself go in?'

'Number three.'

'What happened?'

'Out first ball; bowled by Billy Green. A sneaker that bounced a couple of times before it hit the stumps.'

'What did Jessop have to say about that?'

'When he got back in the changing room he threw his bat

into a corner and said as far as he was concerned the new stand in the County ground could bloody well burn down and the sooner the better.'

Delighted by this authentic voice from the sporting past and feeling that his exploration of the village was already proving a success Hooky took his leave of the ancient and moved on.

Not far from the cricket ground Sweeting Church stood on a gentle rise so that the churchyard and the sunken road that ran by it commanded a view of most of the village.

Hooky was not a formally religious person. Of all the quirks and capers that the human kind gets up to the posturings invented in the name of religion seemed to him to be the oddest; it always struck him as incongruous that when men wish to speak to God they should dress up like women; nevertheless he was Englishman enough to know in his bones that you can never properly get the feel of an English village until you have visited the church and the churchyard round it.

This was where the rude forefathers of the hamlet slept; Hooky had no doubt that some of them had been very rude indeed, although it didn't say so on their tombstones, many of them long since lichened over and well nigh indecipherable.

When he was halfway through the churchyard he was startled by the sudden realisation that a figure was seated on one of the vaults. A woman. Completely immobile, watching him. Her presence there was so unexpected that it made him feel creepy. And with the feeling of creepiness came the instinctive certainty of who she must be.

Just to prove how right his instinct was he very nearly asked her there and then for the recipe for goose balm. He was too scared to do this and so took refuge instead in the Englishman's unfailing topic.

'A nice day,' he ventured.

The wise woman didn't seem impressed by Hooky's qualities as a weather assessor.

'That'll rain by nightfall,' she told him authentically. 'There's a storm brewing. The hoddimedods are out.'

She was obviously not disposed to have further conversation, and Hooky was glad enough to go on his way. The encounter had been oddly disturbing. (What the hell is a hoddimedod, anyway? he wondered as he walked off; and a storm brewing?) He scanned the inoffensive-looking sky; he couldn't see any signs of a storm.

In the lane running alongside the churchyard a solitary car was parked. Hooky idly speculated about it; if any activity was going forward in the parish church at a quarter to twelve on an ordinary weekday morning there was more life in the Establishment than he had imagined.

By half past twelve Hooky's inspectional tour of the village of Sweeting and its environs was finished; he was astonished, and even alarmed, at the distance he had covered. 'My God, this walking lark is becoming a habit,' he warned himself. 'If I'm not careful I shall be an addict.'

He was now at the far end of the village, in the lesser and inferior parts of Lower Sweeting. A man from Sweeting proper might occasionally deign to have a word with a Lower Sweeting-ite, but not often; a Lower Sweeting woman always referred to anyone from the main village as 'that toffee-nosed lot up there'; when the two factions encountered one another in a darts match blood as well as beer was apt to flow.

Blissfully unaware of these undercurrents of neighbourly love, Hooky was interested only in the comforting fact that he had landed up opposite the Lower Sweeting dispensary of comfort and hope, the Plough.

Outside the Plough P.C. West in uniform was wheeling his bicycle.

Catching sight of Hooky, the constable halted and fired a ranging shot.

'Making the round of them, then?'

'A habit of mine,' Hooky pointed out, 'flitting innocently from bar to bar.'

'What some people call pub-crawling.'

'Crawl!' Hooky cried indignantly. 'I've walked miles.'

'That's because you choose to. Your idea of a bit of fun; and anyway you haven't anything better to do – you wouldn't have, being a Private Eye, would you? I have to walk miles every day in the performance of my duty.'

Hooky had to move to one side to let the bus go by; P.C. West watched it with the malevolent glance which he bestowed on most things in the world. '*Progress,*' he said.

The tone of voice puzzled Hooky; his statement that he couldn't see anything wrong in having a bus service brought sardonic pleasure to the village policeman.

' 'Course you can't,' he said. 'You come from London, you do. Up there they can't see anything except who's going to get into the next Honours List (don't make me laugh) and whether the next chairman of some national board or other is going to get fifty-five thousand a year, or only fifty thousand. That's a nice point, that is; that's something us chaps on the beat are passionately interested in, I can tell you. A bus service? I'll tell you what's wrong with a bus service. There used to be six trains a day, three in the morning, three in the afternoon, from here to the market town. And the same back again. Serving five stations on the way. That was jobs for a score and more men and travel in comfort for everybody and a choice of six times. Then along come one of these fifty-thousand-a-year London gentlemen with his axe – never been near Sweeting in his life, of course, nor never will be – what's all this, he says, sitting comfortably on his backside in his office and looking at a map, country people being properly served by a local train service? Can't have things like that going on. So now the railway is closed; there's grass growing all along the track; there are squatters in two of the signal boxes; instead of six trains a day a bus goes twice and not at all on Sundays. No conductors, of course. Pay as you enter and unpleasantness if you haven't got the exact fare, some union or other is talking about making it against the rules for drivers to give change. Like I said – progress.'

'Everybody ought to be fitted out with skateboards,' Hooky suggested brightly, 'and whizz about like anything. Individual transport.'

'Not in my village they won't be,' P.C. West assured him. 'I won't have skateboards whizzing about in Sweeting, in spite of interfering strangers from outside.'

When Hooky finally entered the Plough it took him only the shortest possible time to realise that its honest-sounding title ought to be changed to *Ichabod* and draped in black crêpe. The glory had indeed departed. Even as he went in one of the misguided inhabitants of Lower Sweeting was in the act of feeding a coin into a mechanical contraption which immediately began to belt out an unmelodious maelstrom of sound. Wherever chrome or plastic could be used they were. The art of the cellarman had been forgotten and King Keg reigned.

Thirst and hunger, honestly acquired after his morning's perambulation, forced Hooky to go through the motions of worship in this desecrated temple. He drank a pint of uninspired beer and ate something called a 'ploughman's lunch', consisting of a piece of cheese which any self-respecting mouse would have scorned, a hunk of that white bread specifically designed to promulgate cancer and a minute piece of the E.E.C. butter mountain almost impenetrably wrapped up in paper.

He was only too glad to be out in the fresh air again. There were no signs yet of the wise woman's threatened storm; the sky was still clear and, feeling the necessity of forgetting his unfortunate experience in the Plough, Hooky was happy to curl up under a convenient hedge and sleep in the warm sunshine.

He slept longer than he had intended to. When he awoke he felt stiff and most of the warmth had gone out of the sun. To restore his circulation and to work the stiffness from his limbs, Hooky strode out boldly, fetching a wide circle right round the perimeter of the village before finally ending up at the Arms late in the afternoon.

The Arms was a welcome sight; coming back to its friendly sanity after the midday horror of the Plough was like coming home after disastrous travel in foreign parts.

Mrs Old sought him out. 'Mr Furlong asked me to tell you goodbye,' she informed him.

'Goodbye?'

'He went off today, on the bus.'

Hooky was surprised. 'He didn't say anything to me yesterday about leaving,' he said.

'Nor to me, neither,' Martha Old agreed. 'I did think he seemed a bit quiet when he came in yesterday afternoon, thoughtful like; but then that's the sort of gentleman he is, I thought. But there wasn't a word about leaving. So this morning when he suddenly said he was packing up, well you might say it came as a bit of a shock. I thought he was going to be here some days yet from the way he had been talking. In fact it was only the day before yesterday that he told me he would be staying on for a while.'

'He probably ran out of interesting birds to watch,' Hooky surmised. 'No more tufted tail twisters about.'

Mrs Old gave a dutiful laugh, but her thoughts seemed to be elsewhere. 'There wouldn't be any other reason why he should decide to go in such a hurry, would there, Mr Hefferman?' she asked.

'Not that I know of,' Hooky assured her, 'but, bless your life, Mrs O, there's nowt so queer as folk, people get up to all sorts of odd things.'

'That's just what I'm afraid of,' said Martha Old thoughtfully . . .

Hooky was tired after his hours of exercise in the fresh air; he told himself that he would have to be careful lest the bad habit of walking got a hold on him – a walking addict, he thought in alarm. God save us, what a thing to become.

He went up to his room, kicked off his shoes and lay on the bed, smoking. He mused on his fellow guest's abrupt departure. No doubt it was a little troublesome to her but the good Mrs Old seemed unduly put out by it, he thought; from his own point of view one favourable aspect of the matter was that the departed bird-watcher had forgotten to collect the paperback which he had lent to Hooky and which Hooky now picked up thankfully to read.

Double Fault gave every evidence of being a rather better than average horse out of the comedy-thriller-detective stable. A useful nag for a gallop across oblivion country. As he read his way into the story, Hooky was relieved to find that it bore singularly little relation to reality. Who the hell wants art to echo life anyway? he thought; the business of art is to offer escape from reality; life made harsh enough noises itself without having to listen to echoes of the damned thing.

Halfway through the first chapter of the book the principal character made his appearance and Hooky found his name mildly surprising. He was still pondering the odd little matter when instinct told him that it was time to attend the stirring of the waters; that the hour had come when the halt, the maim and the blind, the fate-buffeted and travel-stained, the pilgrims seeking solace and sustenance who had been waiting for the Angel of Mercy to give them the nod, could enter – in other words, it was opening time for the bar.

Before long a man Hooky had not seen before came in and gave his order. 'Looks in need of a drink,' Hooky thought, eyeing the newcomer with the delighted interest with which he observed the innumerable oddities and quirks of his fellow men.

The stranger gave his very sensible order. 'Large Scotch and water, no ice.'

'Very good, Mr Donaldson,' Old answered, for the newcomer was no stranger to him. 'Been visiting Sir Frederick, I expect?'

Donaldson laughed. 'More or less,' he said.

Hooky wondered how you visited a person more or less. The accountant swallowed half his drink at a gulp and went on, 'It's a bit of a nuisance; well, more than a bit because I want to get off home. Sir Frederick said three-thirty, so of course I was there at three-thirty. On the dot. It doesn't do to be unpunctual with Sir Frederick; but he wasn't there. The butler said he had gone out soon after lunch and was sure to be back soon. So of course I waited. This was three-thirty, mind you, and I waited till six.'

'And Matton still wasn't back?' Hooky asked.

Donaldson turned and looked at the questioner whom hitherto he had hardly noticed.

'This is Mr Hefferman,' Charles Old, a polite man, explained, 'as is staying at the Arms for a few days.'

The accountant was not interested in a visitor staying at the Arms for a few days. 'No, Sir Frederick still isn't back,' he answered sharply; 'although I really don't know what his movements have got to do with you.'

'Elephant's child,' Hooky answered amiably.

Donaldson stared at him. 'I beg your pardon?'

Hooky laughed. 'The late Rudyard K.,' he explained. 'Out of fashion these days, but packed full of good things. In this case it was the elephant's child who was stuffed with it.'

'Stuffed with what?'

' 'Satiable curiosity, the same as I am. I just wonder about things.'

'I'm sure you find it very interesting,' Donaldson said; he turned his back on Hooky and told the landlord, 'I'll have the other half, Old, then I'll go back to the house once more and if Sir Frederick still isn't back I'll go off home. We've got people coming in this evening and I'm cutting it fine as it is.'

Presently the memory of Martha Old's morning promise came back in force to Hooky. Cold roast beef, baked potato, Double Gloucester, was too potent a charm to be resisted; he drained his glass and made his way toward the minute dining room. On his way he caught sight through a window of a car drawn up outside the Arms. Presumably it belonged to the man still in the bar and Hooky found it interesting.

He ate his meal with *Double Fault* propped up against the cruet stand. The story, with its oddly named hero, did not seriously distract his attention from as good a meal as any gastronome might hope for – simple, but everything supremely good of its kind. Hooky ate with a sort of reverent appreciation whilst the storm which the wise woman had foretold began to rumble outside

CHAPTER NINE

'Anything funny –'

The storm raged during the evening and for most of the night but blew itself out towards morning; the storm belonged to yesterday; on the day after only the traces of it remained to be cleared up. The wind had dislodged some tiles from the roof of the Village Hall and had blown down one of the six large elm trees that stood like guardians at the far end of the cricket field. Various sheds and temporary structures throughout the village had suffered and leaves and small branches were scattered everywhere. Sweeting reckoned that it had been 'a rare old blow', and Hooky, sitting at the breakfast table, realised how wrong he had been to doubt the weather forecasting abilities of the wise woman.

Breakfast had been up to Mrs Old's generous standard, and Hooky, who only too often started the day with a couple of aspirins and a look out of the window, had enjoyed every mouthful of it.

With his second cup of coffee he lit what, in spite of strong opposition from the post-luncheon and post-prandial contenders, he always maintained to be the best cigarette of the day.

He smoked with slow deliberation, sipping his scalding hot coffee the while. My Lady Nicotine exercised her patent magic upon him. E might indeed equal MC^2; Hooky did not deny the validity of the equation; but, just at the moment, he couldn't get worked up about it. The world probably was correctly described as a mechanism speeding inexorably towards the cosmic junk heap but – a good breakfast inside him, the first cigarette of the day in his lips – Hooky felt sure there were still interesting things to be seen on the way.

There stirred within him powerful memories from his true

environment. He began to feel that he had dwelt in the tents of Kedar long enough and that it was time to end his voluntary exile and to get back to his home pastures; and home pastures for Hooky Hefferman meant the roar and bustle, the untidiness and warmth and friendliness, of that slatternly old lady among capital cities – London town.

Home pastures meant El Vino's and the dark-eyed Rosie in the Magpie in Mercer's Court.

El Vino's, amusing and alive with the gossip, rumours, lies and boastings of the street, sardonically surveyed by the figure of Lewis, immovable at his chosen end, the inevitable bottle of claret in front of him. The Magpie and dark-eyed Rosie's standard welcome: 'And what have you been up to, Mr Hefferman? Don't tell me; I'm too young to hear' – *Tempus abire adest*, Hooky thought, pleasantly surprised that even that much of an expensive sojourn at Eton should remain with him.

In the course of the morning he learnt from Mrs Old the time of the village bus. 'You'll have to go on the same one that Mr Furlong caught yesterday,' she told him; and it was this fact of the other visitor's departure which provided the next point of interest, for whilst Hooky and Martha Old were talking together P.C. West came in.

'I think you've got another gentleman staying here, Mrs Old,' he said. 'I'd like a word with him please.'

'Mr Furlong? He left yesterday.'

'Gone, has he?' The constable seemed slightly disconcerted. 'Were you expecting him to go, or was it sudden like?'

'Well, actually, Mr West, it did come as a bit of a surprise. I was expecting Mr Furlong would be staying on for a few more days.'

'What made him change his mind then?'

'I'm sure I don't know. I don't ask my guests *why* they do things, Mr West; that's their business.'

'Decided to go in a hurry, though, did he?'

'Like I've told you. I had the impression that Mr Furlong meant to stay on a bit; but I could have been wrong, of course'.

'Was there anything funny about his going?' the constable asked. 'Anything you noticed?'

'What kind of funny? What should I notice about a guest leaving the Arms?' Mrs Old replied. 'He just went.'

Hooky was watching Martha Old as she made this reply and he couldn't help thinking that if ever a woman looked uneasy about the brave words coming out of her mouth the landlady of the Arms did at that moment. *What the hell gives here?* he wondered; aloud he said:

'What do you want to see the little bird-watcher for? Any golden eagles missing?'

P.C. West remained singularly unamused. 'I understand as this Mr Furlong called to see Sir Frederick Matton at Leys the day before he left,' he said.

'Maybe they were buddies together in the bird-watching business.'

'You think so?' the constable asked.

'I didn't say I thought so, my dear old law enforcer. I said *maybe*. I advanced a possible hypothesis.'

'Is that how you Private Eyes go on, talking like that?'

'Some of the time. But if you want to know what they talked about you can always ask Sir Frederick, can't you?'

'My word, you do think up some brilliant ideas, don't you?'

'It seems a sensible suggestion,' Hooky admitted modestly.

'It may seem sensible to you,' P.C. West said, 'but that's because you don't know what goes on in the village. You're just poking your nose in. Sir Frederick Matton left his house in the early afternoon yesterday and hasn't come back since, so it wouldn't be very easy for me to ask him, would it?'

'Do you mean to say that Matton is missing?'

'I didn't say as he is missing. That's how you amateurs go on, jumping to conclusions. All I'm saying at the moment is that Sir Frederick left the house in the early afternoon yesterday and hasn't been seen since; and I would have liked a word with Mr Furlong to see if he could throw any light on the matter.'

'Well, I'm sorry I can't help you, Mr West,' Mrs Old said,

'but there it is. Mr Furlong just isn't here, he left yesterday.'

'I suppose your register is kept properly?'

Martha Old bridled a little. 'Of course it is. The Arms has always been run properly, you know that well enough. What trouble have we ever been to you?'

'All right, all right. I'm only thinking I can get the address of this man Furlong if I want it.'

'You can see the register any time you ask,' Mrs Old answered stiffly.

P.C. West withdrew.

'I try to like people,' Martha Old said, 'because life's nicer that way, but somehow I never have got round to liking Harry West.'

'Not my favourite man,' Hooky agreed.

'Do you suppose Sir Frederick really *is* missing?'

'No, I don't. Why should he be?'

Mrs Old offered no suggestion on this point; after a few moments' thought, and speaking with the air of someone who didn't really want to broach the subject but yet felt compelled to do so, she said, tentatively, 'I wonder what Mr Furlong *did* go to see Sir Frederick about?'

Hooky was wondering about this, too, because certain rather odd remarks which his fellow guest at the Arms had let slip were beginning to stir in his mind. He didn't bother to pin them down accurately at the moment, being more immediately concerned with the intriguing feeling that the woman he was talking to wanted to tell him something and didn't know how to say it.

In the hopes of ultimately getting an egg laid, as it were, he proceeded to apply a little gentle massage.

'Mr Furlong didn't say anything to you about what they talked about up at the big house?' he suggested.

'No, not a thing. And of course I didn't ask. When people come to stay at the Arms what they do is their business and I never try to pry into it.'

'I'm sure you don't,' Hooky said soothingly. 'Not like that troublesome bobby, he'd pry into anything. Whatever can he have meant when he asked you if you noticed anything funny about the way Mr Furlong left?'

'To tell you the truth, Mr Hefferman, it upset me when Harry West asked me that.'

'It did?'

'I didn't tell a lie, though; I didn't say there wasn't anything funny, did I?'

'I'm quite sure you never would tell a lie,' Hooky comforted her. 'What was funny about the way Mr Furlong went?'

'Well, to start with, there was the suddenness of it. Of course anyone can change his mind, but still Mr Furlong had told me so plain that he intended staying on for quite a few days that I couldn't help being a bit surprised when all of a sudden he was asking about the bus. Still, like I said a moment ago, anyone can change his mind and if that had been the only thing I wouldn't have thought anything of it.'

'But it wasn't the only thing?' Hooky prompted gently.

'No, Mr Hefferman, it wasn't. There was the money.'

'The money?'

'I wasn't looking for anything, Mr Hefferman, I do ask you to believe that. Ferreting about is something I never have done and never will. It was just accidental. Mr Furlong was up in his room packing his things and I went up to make sure he understood about the time of the bus and where to catch it – the silly thing is it starts from different places on different days of the week. Well, I went up to make sure as Mr Furlong had got it right and I couldn't help seeing what he was putting into the bit of a suitcase he had with him. I only got a glimpse of it, but a glimpse was enough. I'd never seen a one-hundred-pound note before, Mr Hefferman.'

Hooky realised that the egg had been well and truly laid and instinct told him that it might turn out to be an extremely interesting one.

'A one-hundred-pound note?' he queried.

'And not *one*, there were quite a lot of them.'

'A lot of one-hundred-pound notes,' Hooky said dreamily. 'What a lovely sight. Are you sure about this?'

'Quite sure, Mr Hefferman. I only got a quick glimpse but it was all I needed. And what I saw was Mr Furlong putting a wad of one-hundred-pound notes into his suitcase.'

'Lucky little Mr Furlong.'

'And now there's Harry West going on about Sir Frederick being missing – '

'He didn't actually say "missing".'

'Well, not being at home, anyway. I hope there's nothing funny going on, Mr Hefferman. I wouldn't like anyone from the Arms to be mixed up in anything that wasn't right.'

'I'm sure you wouldn't, Mrs Old. I expect there's a perfectly simple explanation of it all, as there is of so many troublesome things, like how to live together in peace and harmony and the existence of evil, and soccer hooliganism and so on, only we just can't think of it at the moment. Could I have a look at your register?'

The visitors' book was produced and Hooky studied it in silence.

'I like the way you put down *English*, Mr Hefferman,' Martha Old said. 'My father was Yorkshire and he wouldn't have any of this "British" business either – *there's Englishmen and there's foreigners*, he used to say, *and I know which I am*.'

Hooky read out the entry immediately above his own: *Mr R. Furlong, Caroline Crescent, Brighton.*

'Have you ever been to Brighton, Mrs Old?' he asked.

'Only once. I think I would have enjoyed it only Old spent the three days we were there at the county cricket ground. I told him I wanted a proper holiday, not to sit watching a lot of grown men play silly games with a bat and ball.' She, too, studied the book. '*Caroline Crescent*,' she said. 'It sounds a nice sort of address, doesn't it? Sort of refined; and yet, in a way, Mr Furlong wasn't the kind of person you would expect to live in Brighton, was he?'

'If his name really *is* Mr Furlong,' Hooky said dreamily.

Mrs Old was startled. 'What on earth do you mean by that, Mr Hefferman?' she queried.

'Nothing probably. It's just the way my stupid mind works.

I get troubled by these blank misgivings of a creature moving about in worlds not realised; like the late Mr Wordsworth; and nobody pays any attention to him nowadays, do they?'

Mrs Old had to confess that she didn't.

Hooky smiled at the honest creature. 'Do you know,' he said, 'I don't think I'll bother about that bus; I think I'll stay on at the Arms for a day or two; would you mind?'

'Mr Hefferman, I wouldn't mind how long you stayed.'

'The number of charming ladies who have told me that,' Hooky said, 'usually late at night, and the trouble it has landed me in – oh dear!'

With thoughts of returning to his home pastures now definitely put on a back burner for a while, Hooky embarked on a leisurely tour of what was rapidly becoming a well-known village to him.

The miniature supermarket which had monstrously ousted and replaced the old village shop advertised reductions in the prices of cigarettes. Hooky was not naïve enough to believe the alluring notices – 5p off and the like – he was inured to the fact that in his lifetime nothing would ever get cheaper; nevertheless he wanted cigarettes so in he went.

Two women were in the shop; one having her purchases checked, the other sitting at the receipt of custom, doing the checking.

The woman doing the checking was, of course, not known to Hooky; but she was very well known to all the inhabitants of Sweeting who regarded her as the most confirmed busybody and prier into other people's affairs ever inflicted on any community.

Mollie Tranter, who was having her purchases checked, disliked her intensely.

'That's four fifty-two, Mrs Tranter. And how's everything at Lodge Cottage, all right?'

Mollie Tranter said that everything at Lodge Cottage was perfectly all right, thank you; and she began to extract the required money from her bag.

'And then, there's the *Star*.'

'The *Star*?'

'The *Soccer Star*. Mr Tranter never came in for it yesterday. I can't think why. He always does come in, every week. He's so keen. Fancy minding so much about a game, I often say; but then, you never know what these menfolk of ours will get up to, do you? And, anyway, your husband goes about so much; he has to go over to Reading quite a bit, doesn't he? And I expect that would make him late, wouldn't it?'

Mollie Tranter didn't say whether going over to Reading would make her husband late or not; she gathered up her change and, basket in hand, walked out.

The shopkeeper turned her attention to Hooky. 'Some people aren't very friendly, are they?' she said complacently. 'Just the cigarettes is it, sir? That's sixty-four.'

'And it says "5p off",' Hooky ventured to point out.

The woman was indignant. She naturally knew who Hooky was. He was one of the two strangers staying at the Arms; what right had he to come into the village shop querying the proper prices of things?

'That's taken off,' she answered sharply. 'That was taken off before ever it was put on.'

Defeated by this remarkable statement and realising that he was up against something formidable, Hooky conceded with a submissive, 'Oh, well, that's all right then.'

The woman smiled; victory, even in small things, was always pleasant. Her eyes lighted on a paper which shouldn't be there.

'And now she's gone and left that *Star* after all!' she exclaimed.

The *Soccer Star* did, indeed, lie there, neglected.

'I'll take it to her,' Hooky offered.

'That's Mrs Tranter, Lodge Cottage.'

'I've met Mrs Tranter,' Hooky said.

The woman snorted. 'Fancy that,' she said. 'Well, that is lucky, isn't it?'

Hooky caught up with the chauffeur's wife just as she reached the Lodge Cottage and his opening words made her turn on the doorstep to face him.

He saw about her the same essentially female attractiveness that he had noticed the moment she had come into the bar of the Cobalt Arms, but when she smiled at him he didn't think her smile was an altogether happy one.

'You left your paper behind.'

'Oh, thank you. It was that woman in there, she always talks so much.'

'Village shopkeepers tend to gossip,' Hooky suggested.

'Gossip is right,' Mollie Tranter declared. 'She knows everybody's business, that one. Did you bring the paper along specially? That was very kind of you.'

'Always happy to be of service to a lady,' Hooky assured her, 'and I was wondering if you had heard whether Sir Frederick had turned up yet?'

'Turned up yet?'

'He left the house sometime yesterday afternoon and hadn't come back by eleven o'clock this morning – but then, of course, you probably know this already.'

Mollie Tranter stared at him without speaking for some seconds and Hooky began to realise that she didn't know.

He decided to fly a kite. 'I thought, perhaps, that when your husband came back from Reading yesterday afternoon – ' He left the kite flapping in the air.

'Roger didn't get back from Reading yesterday afternoon,' the woman said slowly. 'Something must have kept him there.'

CHAPTER TEN

Six honest serving men

It would have been difficult to say exactly how it came about, but gradually Sweeting became aware that not only was Sir Frederick absent from Leys, but that Roger Tranter, the Leys chauffeur, was not to be found at Lodge Cottage.

The news pleased and displeased the village in almost equal proportions. Those who were always ready to believe in skulduggery and machinations in other people's lives and who took a vicarious delight in reading about them were disappointed; those who preferred people to behave normally and life to run on uneventful lines were relieved. 'What could be more natural?' the no-histrionics-please-we're-British faction said. 'Sir Frederick is away on some big business deal and obviously he has gone in his own car with his own chauffeur.'

It was a point of view which P.C. West was inclined to adopt, as he explained to Charles Old in the bar of the Cobalt Arms. 'It looked a bit funny at first, Matton going off so sudden and without a word to anyone; but you know what these big international men are, on the telephone all day long, something comes through unexpected and away they go. If he hadn't gone off in the car I might have worried a bit. He could have been lost in Sweeting Bog; or something of that sort; but I can't waste my time bothering about rich men who choose to go off all of a sudden in their chauffeur-driven cars.'

'So you don't suspect Mr Furlong of anything any more?' Hooky put in.

'Whoever said anything about suspecting anybody?' the constable demanded.

Hooky smiled amiably. 'I thought the traditional thing was for the police to suspect everybody,' he said.

'Did you? Well, if it comes to that I *do* suspect everybody. All day long I hear people telling me what good citizens they are, wouldn't dream of hurting anybody or doing anything wrong, so where do all the muggings and rapes and burglaries come from, I wonder?'

'And which do you think Mr Furlong was guilty of? Mugging, rape, or burglary?'

'Ah, now we are being funny. Proper Private Eye stuff, this is. Trying to take the mickey out of the regular force. I wouldn't try to be too clever if I was you, Mr Hefferman. You might easily say something that could get you into trouble. Guilty? I never said Mr Furlong was guilty of anything. The butler up at Leys was a bit worried about Sir Frederick not coming back when he was expected and I told him I'd make a few enquiries and see if I could find out anything. All I could find was that someone staying at the Arms left a bit unexpected. Which he is quite entitled to do. And a pity some other people staying there don't do the same.'

When the door closed behind the policeman, Old said soothingly, 'That's Harry West all over; I don't say as he isn't good at his job, but he just can't help saying the sharp thing. You don't want to take no notice of that, Mr Hefferman.'

'The arrows of spite strike ineffectually against the armour of good humour.'

'Is that your Chinese friend again?'

'The same,' Hooky said. 'Chu-Ling. How clever of you to recognise him. The old gentleman has a habit of picking up his celestial hammer and hitting the philosophic nail bang on its inscrutable head. I feel much too good-humoured today to let Mr Harry West ruffle me.'

The door opened and Donaldson came in.

'What news on the Rialto?' Hooky greeted him.

'Still full of curiosity?' the accountant asked. 'Still being inquisitive about other people's affairs?'

'I keep six honest serving men
(They taught me all I knew)
Their names are What and Why and When
And How and Where and Who,'

Hooky quoted.

'Well, you can give 'em a rest as far as this village is concerned. I've just come from Leys and apparently Sir Frederick went off suddenly in his car yesterday and no one knows when he will be back.'

'I wonder where he has gone to.'

'And I wonder why you should wonder. I can't see that it has got anything to do with you. But if you really want to know I'll make a guess and say Paris. The firm has got big interests over there.'

'So everything's hunky-dory, eh?'

'Well, at least the local bobby won't be going round talking about search parties any more.'

'It must be a relief for you, too,' Hooky suggested, 'having spent all day yesterday waiting for him.'

'Half the day,' Donaldson corrected him. 'Three-thirty I was due to see him and I got to the village a minute or two before that.'

'Punctuality itself,' Hooky said admiringly, 'a virtue I have never been able to cultivate – not that I've been much good at any of the others either.'

'I believe you,' Donaldson said; 'but if you were in my line you would find you would have to cultivate a few virtues – punctuality and minding your own business among them.'

'I shall return to London tomorrow suitably chastened.'

'You're leaving Sweeting tomorrow?'

'I might, duty calls.'

'I'm astonished you can recognise her voice,' the accountant said as disagreeably as he could.

Hooky laughed. '*Touché*,' he admitted without any rancour.

*

Next morning Hooky put his lighter away in his pocket and expelled the first lungful of satisfying smoke.

'If I stayed here any length of time, Mrs O,' he said, 'I'd get a tummy on me like an alderman the way you feed me up.'

'Nonsense, Mr Hefferman; you're a good figure of a man, and that's a thing every woman likes to see – as I make no doubt you have found out.'

'Finding out what every woman likes has been very entertaining and very expensive,' Hooky said. 'Men are unwise and curiously planned – did you know that, Mrs O?'

'I'm fifty-two years of age,' Martha Old replied, 'and I guessed as much.'

A few minutes later, while busy clearing the breakfast table, she said, 'Is that right you are leaving us today, Mr Hefferman? My husband said you mentioned something about it in the bar yesterday evening.'

'The thought did cross my mind.'

'Well, I'm sure you have plenty of business to get back to.'

Hooky did his best to look as though he deserved the compliment, but the truth was that he had no business to go back to except the business of waiting for business, and the allied business, always dear to him, of observing the quirks and oddities of his fellow men and the tangled mess they were only too likely to make of their affairs. The suspicion was beginning to stir faintly in his mind that he might get as much joy in that direction if he stayed where he was for a day or two instead of hurrying back to London.

'If you are thinking of leaving,' Mrs Old advised, 'remember, when you go for the bus, it's the other day today.'

Hooky sought elucidation of this curious statement.

'It's day and day about,' Mrs Old explained, in splendid amplification of the mysterious, 'and if you aren't careful you forget which is which. Mondays, Wednesdays and Fridays it starts from outside the Arms here; on the other days you have to go to the far end of the Green to catch it.'

Hooky considered this and said that on the whole he was

inclined to give the bus a miss for a day of two longer.

'Oh, I am glad to hear you say that,' Mrs Old exclaimed. 'And Old will be pleased, too. He enjoys talking to you, Mr Hefferman; he says you remind him of your aunt – '

'God forbid!' Hooky said piously.

'Not *like* her, of course. He means you remind him of the old days; he's a great one for the old days is Old; but people have always said that, haven't they? They've always said yesterday was better than today.'

'Maybe it always has been. Maybe there was Paradise once. Green and cool and innocent. The morning of the world. And then we got too clever. Some fool invented money and when there wasn't enough of it to pay the wages at the Tower of Babel the whole bang shoot fell down and we've been trying to pick up the bits ever since.'

'It's the money that worries me,' Martha Old declared.

'The one-hundred-pound notes?'

'I wish I hadn't seen them. A lot of money means a lot of trouble in my experience.'

'There's often an innocent explanation of the oddest-looking things.'

'I'm sure there is. You think it was all perfectly all right then, don't you?'

'Oh, not necessarily,' Hooky said cheerfully. 'Don't let's be pessimistic. There may be a most diverting little story to be dug out. After all, a wad of one-hundred-pound notes wants a bit of explaining, doesn't it? It seems almost certain that Mr Furlong got the money from Matton. I'll make a guess and say that Sir Frederick Matton is not in the habit of scattering one-hundred-pound notes around, so why should he shower a handful of them on our little Mr Furlong?'

Mrs Old didn't know.

'Suppose Furlong had come across something out of the past. Not necessarily criminal – though, of course, it might be – but something indiscreet perhaps, which Matton didn't want noised abroad – '

Martha Old began to be more worried than ever. 'Oh dear,' she said slowly, 'blackmail – '

'What dreadful words you use, Mrs O!' Hooky exclaimed. 'Still, if that's the way things went it might indeed have looked like blackmail to Sir Frederick; and now off he has gone, hot foot, to consult his lawyer and to do something about it. I don't think he's the sort of man to take a thing like that lying down.'

'Oh dear, oh dear,' Mrs Old shook her head. 'The things that go on in this village!'

'Intriguing, isn't it?' Hooky said, in great good humour. 'Much too intriguing to be worrying about where the bus starts from for a day or two. So, like I said, I'm afraid you won't be getting rid of me just yet, Mrs O.'

'I'm pleased about that, Mr Hefferman, and I do hope as everything turns out all right.'

'It seldom does,' Hooky assured her cheerfully, 'and it's much more fun when it doesn't.'

Leys was an architectural eyesore of a place built in the heyday of Edwardian vulgarity; it was an epitome of the age it belonged to, having cost a lot, being soundly built of first-rate materials, and totally lacking any sort of refinement or distinction.

The manservant opened the door to Hooky and Hooky smiled in his friendliest fashion at him.

'Sir Frederick Matton in?' he enquired amiably.

Sir Frederick was not in; indeed he was away.

'Away?' Hooky sounded sorry. 'Oh dear, I was hoping to have the pleasure of calling on him. I think he knows my aunt, the Honourable Mrs Page-Foley.'

Hooky, of course, didn't think anything of the sort; but he was wise in the ways of superior servants and he knew the beguiling effect that a title or two could have on them, to say nothing of a hyphen.

Drage, Sir Frederick's manservant, was astonishingly quick, like all his tribe, at making social assessment of a stranger. This one looked all right to him; and moreover he had an Honourable for an aunt. And an Honourable with the right sort of name.

'Sir Frederick will be back some time later today perhaps?' Hooky suggested.

'I'm afraid I can't tell you, sir; indeed I wish I knew.'

'I heard in the village that he had gone away unexpectedly, but I thought I had better come up on the off chance. Mrs Page-Foley will be very disappointed if I don't manage to see him; and anyway, you know what village gossip is.'

'Indeed I do, sir. What were they saying exactly?'

'Oh, it was just something I heard in the pub. I'm staying there for a night or two. The Cobalt Arms. Nice little place. I expect you know it.'

'I have been in it, of course, sir. Occasionally. It doesn't do to go too often. Not in my position. That would be Mr Old saying something, would it, sir?'

'No, not Charlie Old. He's a good fellow, isn't he? I like him. And, by an odd coincidence, he used to be in service with my aunt once. He knows how things ought to be done. Just as you do. So I expect you get on well together. No, it was a man called Donaldson who came in –'

'That's Sir Frederick's accountant, sir.'

'I believe you,' Hooky said. 'He looked like an accountant.'

Drage smiled. It was not a remark he could make himself, but he was glad that it had been made. He didn't like Donaldson.

'And what did Mr Donaldson have to say, sir?' he asked.

'Oh, just that he had an appointment to see Sir Frederick in the afternoon. Three-thirty, I think he said. You told him that Sir Frederick had gone out. Unexpectedly, I think you said; and ought to be back soon. According to Donaldson's story – but of course people exaggerate like the devil, don't they? – he hung on till six and then gave it up as a bad job. He seemed to think it odd that Sir Frederick should have told him to report to the house at half past three and then not be there.'

'May I ask your name, sir? It's always a pleasure to meet a gentleman from what I like to call the old life.'

'Hefferman. There were two of us at Eton, myself and a distant cousin. I naturally acquired a nickname' (Hooky pointed to his nose), 'but for better or worse Hefferman it is; and yours?'

'Drage, Mr Hefferman,' the manservant answered; he was delighted to hear about Eton, it confirmed his social diagnosis. 'I've been in service since I was fifteen. And my father was before me. So what you just said a moment ago about knowing how things ought to be done is right. Unfortunately things aren't done like that any more, are they? So we just have to make the best of what we've got. I don't mind telling you, sir, that I thought it was a bit odd about Mr Donaldson.'

'What was odd about him?'

'Well, he wasn't expected. Sir Frederick hadn't said a word to me about anybody coming. And he always does. That's one thing he's very particular about, if he's expecting anybody to call he always lets me know. But, of course, when Mr Donaldson said he had been told to come at three-thirty I explained that Sir Frederick had gone out unexpectedly and I showed him in to the study.'

'Unexpectedly?'

'Not as unexpectedly as all that, no. When he was down here Sir Frederick would quite often go out for an hour after lunch and take a walk round the estate. He would usually let me know he was going and give me an idea of how long he would be: *"Shan't be long," or "Back for tea at four-thirty sharp,"* something of that sort. What was really unexpected was that he hadn't come back by six o'clock, which was when Mr Donaldson left, and the way he went on anyone would have thought it was my fault. I as good as told him it wasn't my place to dictate to Sir Frederick when he comes in and out.'

'And he hasn't come back yet?'

'Well, I'm not so worried about that now as I was that late afternoon and evening. Funny things can happen to people these days. And then there's always Sweeting Bog, so when seven o'clock came and he still wasn't back I don't mind admitting I *was* worried. I sent down to the Lodge to see if they knew anything. And Tranter – that's the chauffeur, Mr Hefferman – wasn't there. I knew he had gone over to Reading in the morning, but I also knew he was expecting to be back before dark. Roger Tranter *and* Sir Frederick both absent, I thought, well that's funny; that can't be a coincidence. Again when next morning came and neither of them had turned up I knew it wasn't a coincidence. On his way back from his walk after lunch Sir Frederick must have seen Tranter in the village – just back from Reading – and decided on the spur of the moment to go off somewhere, that's how I reckoned it.'

'A bit sudden, wouldn't you say?'

Drage laughed. 'I'm used to that,' he said. 'I didn't put any importance to that. That's what Sir Frederick is like. I've known him decide in half an hour to fly to New York. And as for flipping over to Paris, that's nothing.'

'But he has been away for the night.'

'And probably will be two or three more nights yet. I'm expecting to hear on the phone any minute.'

'What does he do about night things on these sudden trips?'

'Bless your life, Mr Hefferman, that's no problem. He keeps a complete set of everything he wants in the London flat and the same in the penthouse over the Paris office. He doesn't have to bother with packing, he just gets in the car and goes.'

'Very convenient,' said Hooky. 'I must remember to do that when I'm a millionaire. So now there's no need for the village bobby to worry any more – not that he shows many signs of doing so.'

'I hope he won't,' Drage said with some asperity. 'I hope as Harry West will have the sense to look after village things and leaves Leys alone. If there's one thing Sir Frederick can't abide it's any meddling by the poilce.'

'West came to the Arms to find out why the other guest there had left so suddenly, a Mr Furlong; was he an old friend of Sir Frederick's?'

'That gentleman who called the other day, sir? He's never been here before in his life.'

'Nice little chap,' Hooky said. 'Bird-watcher. Or so he said. Well, if Sir Frederick is away on business I can't see him, can I? My dear old dragon of an aunt will just have to be disappointed.'

'Are you staying long at the Arms, Mr Hefferman?'

'A day or two, maybe. I can't tear myself away. I'm finding life in the country surprisingly interesting.'

'As soon as I hear anything about Sir Frederick's movements I'll give you a ring and let you know, sir.'

When Hooky walked by the cricket field in the course of his perambulation the ancient whose acquaintance he had already made there was standing in rueful contemplation of the two sight-screens, ranged for the winter months alongside the pavilion.

Catching sight of Hooky, he instantly launched into complaining speech.

'And they'll want painting again before next season.' This was said in such an accusing tone of voice that Hooky almost felt responsible for the evidently poor condition of the screens.

'And that means more money. It's all money these days. And what's it worth? You tell me that.'

'I wouldn't recognise the stuff if I saw it,' Hooky assured him, but the Edwardian gentleman seemed very little mollified by this disclosure; he continued to regard Hooky with suspicion.

'Why, when I was a lad,' he went on, 'we had real money. Sovereigns and half-sovereigns. None of this toilet-paper stuff. In those days half a sovereign would see a man through the best part of a week comfortably, now they call it fifty p. and pee's just about right; it won't buy you a bar of chocolate. Mind you, I'm not saying that that man Matton isn't generous. You ask him for a tenner for the club and he'll give it you. Which is very nice in its way, but of course he's no cricketer. He wouldn't know the difference between l.b.w and n.b.g. And from the way people up at Lord's are messing about with the laws of the game I doubt if all of them know it either. Now, the old squire that was here when I first knew the village, he was different. By God, he was; he put first things first, all right. When he wanted to put a new parson into the local living he used to advertise in the *Church Times*: "*Must be a low churchman and a sound opening bat*", so everybody knew where they were.'

'Sir Frederick doesn't play for the village then?'

'I've told you; he's no cricketer; he couldn't play for Little Piddle-in-the-Pisspot, but that chauffeur of his, ah, that's a different story.'

'Roger Tranter can play a bit, can he?'

'He can turn his arm over. That chap's not a bad bowler when he wants to be. If he stuck to it I dare say he could get a trial for the county second eleven – if he stuck to it.'

'But he doesn't stick to it?'

'Well, for one thing he's here, there and everywhere. In the old days there were plenty of men never left the parish all their lives. Unless there was a war and they went off and got killed. But Roger Tranter, he's as much out of the village as he is in it. It's partly his job, of course. Chauffeuring. And then, of course, he's not exactly the sit-by-the-fireside-and-have-a-quiet-evening-at-home type, is he?'

'I suppose not.'

'Very handy, this chauffeuring lark. Get into that big black car of Matton's and go off anywhere you like. Reading, for instance.'

'What happens at Reading?'

'Don't ask me, mister. I've got plenty of worries of my own without getting mixed up in other people's. What happens anywhere with a man like Roger Tranter about? They say a poke a day keeps the doctor away and Tranter's one of the healthiest men in Sweeting; and anyway what a man's wife doesn't know she doesn't grieve about, does she? Or maybe she does and just has to put up with it; but when you pick Tranter to play for the village you can never be sure whether he's going to be available or not. And speaking of playing cricket I can see you are interested in the game; I shall be getting up a fund to pay for painting these screens, I don't know if you would care – '

Hooky had the wit to know when he was cornered; with

great good humour he produced his wallet and extracted a pound note.

'One of your bits of toilet paper,' he said, handing it over.

'I'm not saying it doesn't come in useful,' the ancient allowed, tucking the note carefully away in his pocket.

A little way beyond the cricket field Hooky saw Mollie Tranter approaching; he had been turning over in his mind the question of calling to see her at Lodge Cottage and had been trying to think of a valid excuse for doing so. Hooky had a compartment of his mind which he called the E.C.B. – the Earnest Consideration Box – into which he relegated various odd remarks and scraps of conversation which had not been fully explored when first encountered but which struck him as having potential and being worth cultivation.

Rattling about in the E.C.B. for some time had been Mr Furlong's expression of interest on learning that Mollie Tranter was wife to Sir Frederick Matton's chauffeur – '*Indeed, how very interesting*,' the little man had exclaimed. Hooky had wondered at the time, and had increasingly wondered since, what had been so interesting about that fact.

Mrs Tranter saw him coming, and he got the distinct impression that she had no desire to stop and have a chat; but the pavement of the village street was narrow and Hooky ungallantly took a smart step sideways to block her way.

'Nice day,' he said.

The chauffeur's wife was non-committal about the weather; she showed no eagerness to discuss it; she made a slight gesture with the basket she was carrying, as if to underline the fact that she was on her way to the shop.

Hooky was distinctly obtuse.

'We haven't had the pleasure of seeing you in the Arms lately,' he said.

Mrs Tranter's smile was of the most fleeting. 'I don't go there a lot.'

'Plenty of sweet sherry left,' Hooky assured her, 'and lots of gins and tonics.'

'I'm sure you find that convenient,' Mollie Tranter said as she resumed her journey towards the shop.

'Bad luck, mister.' Charlie Dent, who, in the disconcerting manner of small boys, had materialised out of an empty landscape, grinned precociously.

'What are you doing here?'

Charlie ignored the question; grown-ups were always asking him either what he was doing or what he had just done, or what he was about to do; he never told them.

'You drew a blank there, mister.'

'You're an exceptionally unpleasant little boy,' Hooky told him. 'Where's your skateboard?'

Charlie became serious at once; messing about with girls didn't amount to much, skateboards were a different matter.

'That's broken, that is, mister,' he said. 'It wasn't new when I got it and this morning one wheel snapped right off.'

'So we shall all be safe for a bit – until you get another one.'

'Not much chance of that with what happened yesterday.'

'What did happen yesterday?'

'Fat-arse West caught me scrumping in the Rectory orchard and told my dad and my dad gave me a leathering and said I was the biggest bloody nuisance he had ever known.'

'Obviously a man of perception, your father,' Hooky said. 'So he won't be buying you another skateboard for a while, is that it? I expect your friend Mr West will be pleased about that.'

Charlie Dent said something very rude indeed about his friend Mr West and added, 'And, anyway, I know a few things as Westy doesn't, so why should I worry? You going to try to date some other girl friend, mister?'

'Go back to your father,' Hooky advised, 'and ask him to repeat the dose.'

Charlie grinned. 'Better luck next time,' he said, and ran happily off.

Back at the Arms, Hooky discovered Mrs Old in sole charge. 'Every now and again I send Old out,' she explained. 'It does him good to get away from it all for a bit and if he's out of the way I can get on with various things or I can just sit still. Even if two people are very fond of one another they want to be on their own occasionally.'

'You ought to be a marriage counsellor, Mrs O.'

'Ah, marriage – that's a funny business is marriage. If I had a daughter I suppose as I'd want her to get married; but I wouldn't be in a hurry about it. There's a lot of bad apples in the basket.'

'Speaking as one of the very bad apples, I couldn't agree more,' Hooky said.

Martha Old laughed. 'I expect as you would be all right, Mr Hefferman. I think if you gave your word to a girl you'd stick to it. But there are plenty as don't.'

'Round here?'

'No names, no packdrill, as my old dad used to say; but driving a car can come in very handy, can't it?'

Much as he would have welcomed an elaboration on this theme, Hooky realised that he wasn't going to be given one. Direct statement was not the way in which the village communicated; and with her next sentence Martha Old was off on another tack.

'Mr Hefferman, ever since you told me what you did about Mr Furlong I've been worrying over it.'

'What on earth did I say to make you worry, Mrs O?'

'Well, you know, about Mr Furlong knowing something as Sir Frederick didn't want him to know and getting paid to keep quiet about it.'

'Good heavens, you mustn't take that too seriously. That was just a suggestion; a wild surmise, the sort of thing stout Cortez stared at the Pacific with.'

The reference to stout Cortez was lost on good Martha Old. She administered a rebuke to Hooky. 'Well, if you didn't think it was true I don't think as you ought to have said it. And what did you mean by *if his name really is Furlong*? That's another thing that's been worrying me.'

'That's a very interesting psychological point,' Hooky said.

Mrs Old nodded uncertainly. 'Maybe,' she said, 'but to tell you the truth I'm never quite sure what that word means.'

'And believe me, Mrs O,' Hooky assured her, 'there are a

hell of a lot of psychologists aren't sure about it either.' He drew the paperback *Double Fault* from his pocket and opened it at random.

'Take a look,' he invited.

Mrs Old took a look and with a little hesitation began to read out the indicated paragraph: '*Richard Furlong was not disposed to let the matter lie there* – ' She broke off and said, 'Richard Furlong – well, that's funny; that *is* funny that is, him having the same name as the man in the book.'

'Too funny when you come to think of it. I mean too much of a coincidence to be one. But suppose the little man was on his way here to see Matton about some private matter – for the moment we don't know what it is. It *might* have been something on the lines I suggested; but then again it might have been something entirely different. But whatever it is he doesn't want his real name to appear, so he has got to think up an alias for himself. On his way here he is reading this crime story he lent me, *Double Fault*, and the chap in it is called Richard Furlong. That's a nice sort of name, our little chap thinks, that will do me nicely; so when you push the register towards him and invite him to sign himself in down it goes, as bold as brass – *R. Furlong*.'

Martha Old was fascinated. 'Well, fancy that!' she exclaimed. 'And what about the address he wrote down – Caroline Crescent?'

'Do you know, Mrs O,' Hooky said, 'if you keep my room here for me so that I can come back to it I think I'll go to Brighton for a couple of days and take a look at Caroline Crescent.'

CHAPTER ELEVEN

Watchman's Row

The policeman's cottage in Sweeting lay in a somewhat isolated position at the far end of the village, well beyond the cricket ground and the church. Standing on its own, away from the general friendly huddle of village buildings, it seemed to emphasise the fact that its occupier was something of a man apart. That he was choosing a life which would tend to set him apart from his fellows had been drilled into Harry West during his training by an instructor in whom long years in the force had induced a sort of ferocious humour. *Don't go looking for popularity*, he told the class, *because you won't get it; and anyway a popular copper is a no-good copper; don't expect people to like you, because they won't.*

This suited the Sweeting policeman because for his part he didn't like people and he found it no disadvantage that his house should have no immediate neighbours.

The previous occupier had been a keen gardener and had consistently won prizes at the annual Sweeting show. People who win prizes in small communities do so at their peril, and there was a faction in Sweeting who pointed out that the law was likely to turn a blind eye on any misdemeanours of anyone who, in his capacity of judge, had known where to award the rosettes and the prizes.

These considerations didn't apply when West took up his duties in Sweeting; he had a rooted objection to gardening and looked upon any time spent in it as a waste of time.

'And how's the garden looking?' the Inspector asked when he made a visit to see how the new man was settling in.

'I let Mrs West see to that.'

'Ah, keen is she?'

'Well, I'm not anyway. I didn't join the force to grow marrows.'

The Inspector went on his way confirmed in the opinion he had already formed that in Police Constable Harold West they had a conscientious officer but an awkward customer.

Ethel West didn't mind doing what she could in the garden; in fact she rather enjoyed it; the trouble was that what with cooking, keeping the house clean, doing the washing and the necessary shopping expeditions she didn't have much time over; and in any case jobs like cutting the hedge at the bottom of the patch and the heavy autumn digging were too much for her.

She did as much as she was able to and, perforce, let the rest go. She knew from experience that it was no good trying to win her husband round to something he didn't like. She was a little woman whose wishes were seldom sought and even more seldom acted upon; she sometimes allowed herself the liberty of wondering what, if anything, it was that the man she had married *did* like.

Her knowledge of what went on in the village came almost exclusively from her husband. She did her best to make it otherwise. She attended the W.I. meetings on Wednesday afternoons; she sang in the church choir; she took her turn cutting up sandwiches for tea at cricket matches; but she was always on the outside; and always conscious of being so. She was the policeman's wife; and the titbits of gossip, the half-hints and innuendos which the rest of the village fed into the grapevine were largely kept from her.

The view of life in Sweeting which Harry West brought home, when he thought it worth while to treat his wife to an account of it, was inevitably cast in the man's own sardonic vein. He regarded most of his fellow men as villains, proved or potential; those that hadn't yet been found out no doubt soon would be. At the best those who weren't proved knaves were obvious fools, like the chap staying at the Arms.

'Mrs Old was saying in the shop what a nice gentleman he is.'

'If you listen to gossip in the shop you'll hear every sort of silly thing.'

'I thought you always told me to keep my ears open in case I heard anything useful.'

'You aren't likely to hear anything useful about a man who calls himself a Private Investigator.'

'Good gracious! Is that what he is, really?'

'I said that's what he calls himself.'

'What is he here to investigate? About Sir Frederick?'

'You're as bad as the rest of them. What is there to investigate about Matton?'

Ethel West didn't know the answer to that. 'Some people seemed to think it was a bit funny his going away so sudden,' she offered rather lamely.

'*Some people!*' Her husband was away on one of his *bêtes noires*. '*Some people* would say the earth is flat; *some people* would say anything.'

'But didn't you say as Mr Drage up at Leys was worried?'

'Just at first he was worried a bit. Matton had gone out for an afternoon walk and Drage expected him back for tea. When he didn't come and was a couple of hours overdue Drage began to think of Sweeting Bog and a search party; but as soon as he learnt that Roger Tranter and the car were out of the village as well he guessed what had happened.'

'Where has Sir Frederick gone, then?'

'It's a funny thing,' West said with heavy sarcasm, 'but Sir Frederick Matton doesn't always remember to tell the village policeman where he's off to.'

'So I suppose Tranter will be away from home for a bit?'

'It won't be the first time as that has happened,' the policeman said darkly.

'If you ask me I think as Mollie Tranter has a lot to put up with,' Mrs West said, 'that husband of hers is always away in that big car of Sir Frederick's. You can't tell me as he doesn't get up to something on some of these trips.'

'That's none of my business,' West answered. 'I've enough on my plate without trying to look after people's private morals. And in any case what's sauce for the goose is sauce for the gander. No one's making me believe as Mollie Tranter is exactly a saint.'

His wife laughed a little sadly. 'Maybe there aren't any saints,' she said, 'just sinners. That's what you always say, isn't it? So if the gentleman at the Arms isn't investigating about Sir Frederick what is he investigating about?'

'The gentleman at the Arms is not investigating anything – not on my patch, he isn't. He'd do better to get himself a part in one of these fancy films about the force they show on the box instead of meddling where he isn't wanted.'

Mrs West was only too well aware of her husband's poor opinion of TV; she had heard it expressed fifty times, mostly in exactly the same terms, and had no desire to hear it all again; so she chipped in with, 'And the other person staying at the Arms, he's gone now, hasn't he?'

'The bird-watcher? Yes, he's gone.'

'Is that what he was – a bird-watcher? What a funny thing to be.'

'People get up to all sorts of funny games when they've no proper work to do; but I don't suppose it was bird-watching as he went to see Matton about.'

'What did he go to see Sir Frederick about?'

'Perhaps you had better ask your nice gentleman staying at the Arms to find out for you, he's probably gifted with second sight like all these crime-story detectives, Lord Peter Poirot and Father Hercules and Miss Muddle and the rest of them –'

Ethel West, who read all the Agatha Christie and Dorothy Sayers books she could get hold of (but contrived to hide them from her husband), was relieved when the policeman went on, ' – a good job he has gone, too; I mean that other chap at the Arms; Furlong by name; he's one of the interfering lot.'

'Oh dear, what did he interfere in?'

'He interfered with me doing my duty. He's the same as all the Law and Order brigade. Keen as mustard on us coppers doing our job as long as they don't see us at it, and the moment they catch sight of us in action they're up in arms about civil liberties and the rest of the clap-trap. I was telling that young devil Dent about not skateboarding all over the place to the danger of everybody when this chap started to argue the toss. Accused me of insulting him and acting with tyranny and God knows what nonsense. Still, I caught young Dent scrumping in the Rectory orchard yesterday and I took him home and told his dad about it and if I know anything about Ernie Dent he took off his belt and gave the boy a bit of something to remember.'

Ethel West sighed. She had a soft spot in her heart for all mischievous, apple-stealing boys. She would have dearly liked one of her own, but she knew now that she and her husband would never have children. 'I should have thought the Rector could have spared a few apples,' she said; it was a mistake, of course, as she realised as soon as she had made the remark, since it only too easily paved the way for the policeman to launch out into his well-known tirade about the iniquities of the established Church and the futility of all dogmatic religion. Mrs West had heard all this (which was directly contrary to her own most cherished beliefs) so often that she was mightily relieved when the sound of the front-door bell interrupted matters.

'That'll be the milk,' she said. 'I didn't pay him yesterday.'

But it wasn't the milk. Life sometimes stage-manages the tragic farce extremely cleverly and out of the blue contrives a total surprise.

It wasn't the milk. It was a young couple who weren't in the habit of calling at police stations and who were obviously agitated about having to do so.

Was the policeman in? they asked. Yes, he was in, they were told, what was it?

'We must see him,' the young man said, 'it's important,' and the girl nodded in alarmed confirmation.

They were taken inside and Harry West invited them to tell him what it was all about. As they did so he listened with ever increasing excitement to their story . . .

'So you're off to Brighton tomorrow, Mr Hefferman?' Charles Old said.

Hooky held up *Double Fault.* 'I'm taking back Mr Furlong's book to him.'

Donaldson who was also in the bar laughed and said, 'Well, that's really conscientious, that is. I don't think anyone would expect you to do that with a paperback. Furlong, did you say? You mean the little chap who was staying here?'

'The same. Richard Furlong. A nice name, don't you think? Something Anglo-Saxon and earthy about it.'

Donaldson laughed. 'I don't know about earthy,' he said. 'I suppose it's as good a name to go by as any other. What's in a name anyway?'

'Ah, there you have me,' Hooky admitted. 'The Bard didn't know and I'm blowed if I do. A name is a name is a name.'

'Or is it?' Donaldson said, laughing again.

'I tell you one thing, gentlemen,' Old put in from behind the bar, 'Furlong is a better word than all this metre and centimetre stuff. Every Englishman born knows as a cricket pitch is twenty-two yards long. How could it be anything else? Time they start talking about metres up at Lord's we shall know we've really had it.'

'My aunt will be delighted to hear what a splendid traditionalist you are,' Hooky said.

Charles Old smiled. 'Ah, that's your bit of fun, Mr Hefferman. That never did anyone any harm, a bit of fun. When you say "traditionalist" what you really mean is "old fogey", but like Mr Donaldson said a moment ago, what's in a name?'

'I'd never be brave enough to call my aunt an old fogey.'

'And I wouldn't be rude enough to,' Old said quickly. 'Your aunt is one of the old sort. They had the privileges and, my word, they took advantage of them; but, then, they acted right. They did the right things. They had a place and acted up to it. The squire was the squire in those days. Not like it is now – nothing personal, Mr Donaldson,' he added as an afterthought.

'You mean Sir Frederick?' the accountant said. 'Well, of course we all know that he didn't come out of the top drawer. He had to make his own way entirely. Personally I admire him for what he has done. I've had differences and arguments with him, of course. Everybody who works for him has had those; but when you add it all up he's really got somewhere, hasn't he?'

During these laudatory remarks the door had opened and Hooky's acquaintance from the cricket field, the ancient of days, had come in.

'Usual, Charlie,' he said. He watched with a suspicious and supervisory eye whilst his own private pewter pot was lifted down off the shelf and carefully filled with his own particular mixture – a pint of draught beer reinforced by a treble gin.

Hooky looked on in approval. 'Useful sort of drink, that,' he said.

The ancient nodded. 'It's better than a slap on the belly with a wet fish,' he allowed. 'Matton, were you talking about? the man at Leys? And saying he had gone somewhere? Well, he won't get anywhere much now. He's dead.'

The startling announcement he had heard in the Cobalt Arms had made Hooky more than ever anxious to run 'Richard Furlong' to earth and ask him a few questions.

Whenever he thought of the way the news of Matton's death had been broken he was forced to smile. Nature had got art licked every time, he thought. No ranting and raving; no rushing in; no breathless descriptions; no multi-colour stuff. The much more effective black and white approach. And the ancient had got his priorities right. Drink before news any day.

' . . . *he won't get anywhere much now,*' the sardonic old devil had announced. '*He's dead.*'

That created a silence, that word did. Three men were alive and enjoying their drink in the homely, familiar bar and outside the sun was shining; the short, final, word *dead* fell into all this like a heavy stone splashing into a pond.

Hooky happened to be looking at Donaldson at the moment of impact and he found it difficult to assess the expression on the accountant's face.

'Sir Frederick dead?' a shocked Charles Old asked.

The ancient nodded. 'Found in the old shepherd's hut, up by Silverman's Wood, where they go blackberrying.'

'Who found him?' was Hooky's question.

'A couple who told Harry West as they went into the hut in case it came on to rain. We all know what that means, of course. That shepherd's hut comes in very handy for a bit of the old nonsense. As one or two people in the village are well aware. No names, no packdrill.'

'And what had happened to Sir Frederick?' Old asked. 'Dead – how?'

'Shot.' The ancient pushed his now partly depleted pewter pot across the counter. 'I'll have another go of gin in that, Charlie,' he said.

'What a splendid idea,' Hooky said, moving his own glass forward . . . *Death*, he thought, the fell sergeant; the most frequented of all visitors but the least talked about; the daily event which is so seldom seen; the finality; the beyond-which-nothing – or was there something? Did the parsons have a clue after all?

He gave a slight involuntary shiver and the cricketing ancient, noticing it, laughed in sympathy.

'Ay, makes you think,' he said, 'makes you add things up a bit.'

There was a slight pause and then Donaldson said slowly, 'What it's making me think about is the chauffeur. If Roger Tranter isn't away somewhere with Sir Frederick, where is he?'

The three men looked at one another . . .

Hooky thought of all this as the train whisked him down to Brighton. 'I hope not to be more than a couple of days at the most,' he told Mrs Old, 'so you will keep my room for me, won't you?'

'Mr Hefferman, you can be sure of a room at the Arms whenever you like,' Martha Old assured him. 'You'll always be welcome.'

The train curved into Brighton station and walking along the platform to surrender his ticket Hooky sniffed at the sharp, fresh air with appreciation; Doctor Brighton's own prescription, he thought, and a welcome change from the lethargic stuff in Soho.

At the station bookstall he bought a street map of the town and sitting down studied it carefully.

There was no mention of a Caroline Crescent.

Hooky wasn't altogether disappointed; indeed, in one way he welcomed the fact; it had a confirmatory feel about it; if a man gave a false name it was quite likely he would give a false address.

Of course it yet had to be definitely established that a false name had been given. The telephone directory in a nearby kiosk listed four Furlongs with Brighton numbers.

Hooky made a list of the addresses and, street map in hand, set out to do the leg-work – that tedious but essential ingredient of all Private Eye business.

The Brighton Furlongs were all pleasant people and only too anxious to help a polite nephew trying to get in touch with a mislaid uncle, but none of them knew of anybody remotely resembling the man Hooky described.

By four o'clock in the afternoon Hooky had done a lot of walking; had learnt to regard buses as mythical, non-existent things; had chatted up two barmaids (and kept the name of one of them for future reference); and, in regard to his quest, had drawn a total blank. He sat on a seat on the front to consider the matter.

Que faire? was the question, what did one do next? And not to put too fine a point on it, Hooky had very little idea.

There was one faint possibility; but even the optimistic Hooky had to admit that it looked a very slender one indeed.

He drew *Double Fault* out of his pocket. The place he had reached in reading it was marked by a small slip of paper which he had found in the book when it had been given to him and which had evidently been used as a marker before.

Hooky studied it.

It was about two inches long and half an inch wide. It was a bilious pink in colour. It bore the number 337 and underneath, written in ink, the letters S.S.C.A.

It could be a cloakroom ticket; it could be a raffle ticket. As somebody had taken the trouble to keep it more likely the latter, Hooky thought.

He got up from his seat and walked along the front until he came to the town Information Bureau.

The Information Bureau asked if it could help him. Hooky said he hoped so and produced ticket No. 337.

'What's S.S.C.A.?' he asked.

The Info. Bureau knew at once. 'That's Save the Sussex Countryside Association,' it said, 'and they're running a big raffle to help the funds.'

'And this would be one of the tickets, then?'

'Looks like it. But I don't think the draw has been made yet.'

Hooky wasn't particularly interested in the draw. 'How can I get in touch with this Save Sussex lot?' he asked.

'I can give you the address of the secretary,' the Information Bureau said.

'Bless you for ever and a day,' Hooky said.

The Information Bureau smiled.

Dorothea Andrews made an impolite observation about the gas cooker. The cooker was an elderly affair, past its best, and it seemed to delight in displaying its irregularities just when they were least welcome. In the Professor's absence Dorothea had decided to embark on a week of concentrated domesticity and after five days of it she was heartily sick of the extra polishing, cleaning, sewing and cooking she had let herself in for. To resume her tutorials with the Professor would be a treat indeed.

She had thought a great deal about the now famous tutorial when Herbert Aston had told her his story of family trouble and she had been bold enough to take him to task about his part, or lack of part, in it.

Bold? Foolhardy it seemed in retrospect; and she didn't know whether to be amused or embarrassed by the recollection of her audacity.

She opened the oven door to see how the cake was doing.

The cake wasn't doing well at all; for some inscrutable reason the oven refused to get as hot as it should do; yet, as she knew only too well, on another occasion, and set at the same figure, the confounded thing would without warning soar away into temperatures calculated to ruin everything.

She was making the cake (or trying to) for Frances. And that in itself was a disturbing thought. For where was Frances? Frances, aged sixteen, should have been home by now but wasn't. There was probably a perfectly simple explanation of her being late; but, these days, who could be sure?

Dorothea, whose thoughts were often concerned with the Professor, recalled the dreadful story of his niece who had committed suicide; *he that hath children hath given hostages to fortune*: how right wise old Bacon was, she thought a trifle ruefully.

Her Baconian musings were interrupted by the front-door bell. She was mildly surprised. She was not expecting anybody at that time of day; unless, of course, it was Frances who had forgotten her key again . . .

It was not a keyless Frances; and if Dorothea had not been expecting anyone in particular she quite certainly had not been expecting the sort of stranger who now stood on her doorstep. Even before anything was said her face softened into a smile; he ought to have had two others with him, she thought; didn't Musketeers go in threes?

Hooky tipped his cap and asked, 'Are you the secretary of the Save the Sussex Countryside affair?'

'Association,' Dorothea corrected. 'Yes, I am.'

'And you're running a raffle to help the funds?'

'We are. Do you want to buy a ticket?'

'Actually I've got one.' Hooky held up No. 337 pink. 'I was wondering if it belongs to you, or if I can trace whom it does belong to.'

'Well, it won't belong to *me*,' Dorothea said a trifle briskly. 'It wouldn't do for the secretary to have a ticket and possibly win the thing; but may I ask how you come to be interested and how you came by the ticket?'

'I found it used as a bookmarker in a paperback called *Double Fault*.'

'*Double Fault*? – but that's the book I lent to the Professor to take away on holiday with him; and, come to think of it, of course he did buy a ticket. So it will be his.'

'Professor Furlong?'

'Furlong? No, Aston. Professor Herbert Aston.'

'Does he live in Brighton?'

'Of course he does.'

'But not in Caroline Crescent?'

'Caroline Crescent? I don't know a Caroline Crescent. He lives in Watchman's Row. Number nine. Whether he's home yet I'm not sure; for the past few days he has been in France, doing a tour of the châteaux of the Loire country.'

'I doubt it.'

'I beg your pardon?'

'I've a strong suspicion that for the past few days your Professor Aston has been staying at the Cobalt Arms Inn, Sweeting, under the assumed name of Richard Furlong.'

'Why on earth should he be doing that?'

'He was visiting a man called Matton, Sir Frederick Matton.'

'Sir Frederick Matton? I saw that name in the *Telegraph* this morning. Wasn't he found shot in a shed in the woods somewhere?'

'In the woods near Sweeting.'

'What a dreadful affair,' Dorothea said.

'One of the worst things that could have happened to him,' Hooky assured her.

Dorothea disregarded this, as she judged it, ill-considered bit of facetiousness and asked, 'But what on earth has the Professor got to do with it?'

'Just what I should like to find out,' Hooky told her. 'Number nine Watchman's Row, did you say?'

Herbert Aston had just got comfortably settled: cup of newly made coffee within easy reach; footstool in precisely the right spot; pipe newly filled and drawing sweetly;

Viebart's monumental *Dynamic Forces in Western Literature* nicely balanced on his knee.

All this highly agreeable concatention of things had to be disturbed when the doorbell rang.

An earthy exclamation not often heard in the Common Room rose to the Professor's lips as he went into the hall. When he opened the front door and saw who was there he was at first surprised, then faintly disturbed and even mildly annoyed. As far as he was concerned Sweeting was Sweeting and Watchman's Row Watchman's Row; and he wasn't particularly anxious that the twain should meet.

Hooky held up *Double Fault*. 'I've brought back your book,' he said.

Aston had completely forgotten about the paperback, but he was glad to see it.

'You could have posted it,' he said.

'To Caroline Crescent?'

Aston was already beginning to forget the charade of his assumed identity; the recollection of it amused him.

'Perhaps not,' he allowed. 'Well, thank you.' He held out his hand for the book, but Hooky kept hold of it.

'I think we ought to have a little chat,' he suggested.

Aston hesitated for a moment and then rather ungraciously said, 'Well, if you really want to come in perhaps you had better.' He led the way into the study and when both men were seated Hooky handed over the book.

'Silly of me to have forgotten it,' Aston allowed, 'and I'm glad to have it back. Actually it isn't mine; it was lent to me.'

'By Mrs Andrews?'

'You know Dorothea Andrews?'

'You'd be surprised at what I do know.'

'Actually I *am* surprised. About a number of things. How did you find out my name isn't Furlong, for instance? And what business is it of yours, anyway?'

'Listen Prof. – '

'For God's sake don't call me *Prof*; it's an abbreviation I find particularly distasteful.'

'O.K. – '

'And that's not much better. My subject is English, in case you don't know; and if we are to have any discussion I would prefer it to be conducted in that language.'

Hooky laughed. 'Don't get shirty, little man,' he said amiably. 'Matton is the one who would be justified in feeling annoyed.'

Herbert Aston's dealing with *The Times* had, as usual, been confined to the crossword; in all innocence he asked, 'Why should Sir Frederick Matton be annoyed?'

Hooky gave his host a long hard look. Either we've got another Alec Guinness here, he thought, or else he really doesn't know.

'Very troublesome when you get shot,' he said.

'Shot?'

'Sir Frederick Matton was found dead, shot through the head, in a hut in the woods near Sweeting.'

The Professor was visibly shocked by the news. No acting here, Hooky thought.

'Who on earth did that?'

'It's a funny thing,' Hooky said, 'but when somebody gets shot quite a lot of people ask that particular question; and ask it rather urgently.'

Aston drew on his pipe and slowly expelled a cloud of blue, contemplative smoke. 'What you have just told me is very disturbing,' he said at length. 'I'll not deny that. I didn't like Matton and I'll not pretend I did; but there's a difference between not liking a man and hearing that he has been shot dead. This has got nothing to do with me and I don't want to get mixed up in it in any way.'

'You mean you don't want to get *more* mixed up in it.'

'More?'

Hooky sighed; these cloud-cuckoo-land-dwellers, he thought, wrapped up in the obliterating cocoon of academic futility, who think it's all a game; who don't believe that life has got rough edges and can hurt.

'Look, Aston,' he said sharply, 'come down to earth a bit. Take a look at things as the outside world will look at them. As the daily press will. You turn up at Sweeting out of the blue and book in at a pub under a false name. You give out you're a bird-watcher. Maybe you are; anyone can watch birds; but in the Cobalt Arms amongst other things you say, "*I'm after bigger game than birds*".'

'Did I say that?'

'You did. You also said, "*things have a habit of catching up with people*"; then off you go to visit Matton up at his house and when you come back you have abruptly changed your mind about staying on for a few days – which you told Mrs Old you were going to do – and you can't get packed up quickly enough to go. Except, of course, you did give yourself time to put in the bundle of one-hundred-pound notes. The next thing any of us know is first of all that Matton is missing and then that he is found dead, shot. Doesn't it seem likely to you that people might ask a few questions about all that?'

'How on earth did you find out about the money?'

'Never mind how. *How* doesn't matter. There'll be an inquest on Matton and questions will be asked. Suppose you are asked the questions I have just suggested?'

'I shall simply tell the truth. I am a great believer in the truth.'

'You and Pontius Pilate. Well, go on; give me an earful of it. I promise not to laugh. What is the truth?'

So for the first time Hooky heard the story of Notas and Oxtone; of the brother who had died of T.B. and of the girl who had committed suicide.

'When I found out about all that,' Aston said, 'I thought I'd take a hand in it. A wrong had been done and I wanted to put it right. And I must say I rather enjoyed it all.'

These D.I.Y. Don Quixotes, Hooky thought; God save us. What lunacies men get up to.

'So you went to see Matton and told him to cough up – how much?' he asked.

'I asked for fifty thousand pounds; he offered me five thousand. There were certain circumstances which made me think it advisable to accept five thousand.'

'That's about the first sensible thing I have heard you say. I'm surprised you got anything out of him.'

'I had seen Matton before.'

'You had?'

'In the woods. I thought he was the keeper. He came out of the hut up there. A minute or two after the woman had come out.'

'What woman?'

'Mrs Tranter. The chauffeur's wife.'

'Well, well, well,' Hooky said; he was beginning to revise his assessment of the Professor. 'So you put the screws on him a bit – a spot of blackmail.'

'I wish you wouldn't use that word,' Aston said primly. 'Matton used the same phrase, totally without justification.'

'But you let Matton know what you knew?'

'In the course of our conversation he became aware of it.'

'Did you tell anybody else about it?'

'I told Donaldson.'

'The accountant?'

'An unpleasant man. I think he was sent by Matton to size me up, or warn me off, or deal with me in some way. It ended up with my warning him against Matton. I told him that a man who would seduce his chauffeur's wife was hardly the sort of person to trust.'

Hooky laughed. 'I wonder what Donaldson made of that,' he said. He began to wonder very much what Donaldson had made of it . . .

CHAPTER TWELVE

Two interrogations

A police car drew up outside the house in Fox Lane and a C.I.D. man and W.P.C. got out.

The woman who answered the door admitted them to the house reluctantly. She knew who they were and where they were from; she disliked them and the apparatus they represented. She had been on the point of brewing a pot of tea, but she made no mention of this to her unwelcome visitors; she had no intention of offering them anything.

The C.I.D. man spoke with a sort of boisterous bonhomie which sounded about as genuine as an undertaker's sympathy; the W.P.C. sat silent most of the time, a sardonic chaperone.

'Now then,' C.I.D. led off. 'All comfortable, are we? Right. Just a little chat, then, to get a few things settled.'

'I was just about to go out shopping,' the woman lied.

'You were? Fancy that! Shan't keep you long and anyway we are probably saving you money the way prices are today.' He must have thought this witticism funny, for he laughed heartily at it; the W.P.C. smiled dutifully; the woman sat silent.

C.I.D. produced notebook and ball-point pen and said, 'Off we go, then. Name?'

'Rene Walters.'

'That's your full name, is it?'

'I've just said so.'

'Married?'

'I've been married yes; but we've separated.'

'I see. So you live here alone, is that right?'

'Yes, I do – if it's any concern of yours.'

'Ah, don't be like that, Mrs Walters. I'm sure you know who we are.'

'I know who you are, all right.'

'And we know you, so it's mutual, isn't it? There was that little business of shoplifting – '

'That was eighteen months ago. And anyway the case against me was dropped. You know that. There wasn't any evidence.'

'Which was lucky, wasn't it? Well, we don't mind that. Everyone is entitled to a bit of luck. And a bit of help, too. That's what we want you to do now – give us a bit of help.'

'What about?'

'Have you ever heard of a man called Matton, Sir Frederick Matton?'

The woman had often heard about Frederick Matton from the man who drove his cars; but she saw no reason to say so, yet.

'What about him?' she asked.

'He was shot two days ago in a hut in the woods near his home.'

The woman remained silent.

'You didn't know that?'

'Why should I know it?'

'Do you take a daily paper, Mrs Walters?'

'Of course I do. Everybody does.'

'And the news on TV? You listen to that?'

'Yes.'

'And you still want to tell me that you've seen and heard nothing in the last two days about this man Matton being found shot?'

'I didn't say I had seen nothing about it. I just want to know what it has got to do with me.'

C.I.D. laughed heartily again. 'Well, that's a funny thing, isn't it?' he said. 'That's exactly what we want to know as well; so now we're together again, eh?'

'If you say so.'

The woman took a cigarette from a packet in her handbag and lit it. The W.P.C., watching every move, noted how thin the face was and how the blonde hair was already showing dark again at the roots.

'Mrs Walters,' C.I.D. said, 'this man Sir Frederick Matton was murdered. So we are investigating a case of murder. That's why we are here, talking to you. People who help us, help us. People who refuse can find themselves in a very tricky position, believe me. I wouldn't advise you to do that.'

The woman lit the cigarette and blew two plumes of smoke through her thin nostrils.

'*Bastard,*' she thought. Aloud, she said, 'I haven't refused anything. Don't start putting words in my mouth.'

'Oh dear, dear, dear. You'll be talking about police brutality next. I'm not putting any words in your mouth, Mrs Walters. It's words out of your mouth I want. Do you know a man called Roger Tranter?'

'What if I do?'

'I'll ask the questions. And I have just asked you one. Do you know a man called Roger Tranter?'

'Yes, I do.'

'And you know that he is – was – chauffeur to Sir Frederick Matton?'

'Yes, I know that.'

'So a moment ago when you were trying to give the impression that you didn't know anything about Sir Frederick Matton you weren't being quite honest, were you? You know Roger Tranter and you know that he was chauffeur to the man who has just been murdered. How often has Tranter called at this house?'

'How often?'

C.I.D. nodded. 'That's what I asked you. How often? Every time he goes on a job to Reading, he looks in here for his bit of fun, does he? Is that it?'

'He's been here a few times.'

'I'm sure he has. Has he ever spoken to you about the man he worked for – Matton?'

Roger Tranter had often spoken to the woman about his employer, sometimes in the admiration of one villain for another; sometimes, when the two men had disagreed about something, in anger. But she wasn't going to say so. Visits might be proved; what had been said between the two of them could never be proved. The bastards weren't going to get that out of her.

'No,' she said flatly.

'He never said anything about being fed up with his job, or about having had a row with Matton – nothing like that?'

The woman shook her head.

'Perhaps you can't think of anything at the moment,' C.I.D. said. 'We'll be calling again later and maybe you will have remembered something by then. Did Roger Tranter call here three days ago; that's on Tuesday the twenty-seventh?'

'Last Tuesday? He may have done.'

'I asked *did* he?'

'Yes, he did. I remember now.'

'I'm sure you do. Go on trying to remember things, Mrs Walters; it will help us a lot. Did you ever hear Tranter make any threats against Matton, or offer to do him any sort of injury? Can you remember that?'

'No, I can't.'

'You know that Tranter is a violent man?'

'Is he?'

'You didn't know that?'

'I take people as I find them. Mr Tranter was never violent with me.'

'But you knew Mr Tranter had been in prison for violence?'

'If you ask me, a lot of people get sent to prison as shouldn't be.'

'And a hell of a lot more are walking about free as ought to be inside. You can take that from me. What time did Tranter leave here on Tuesday?'

'What time?'

'That's what I asked. Try and remember that.'

The woman paused for a moment or two and then answered, 'Some time between three and four, I suppose.'

'Sometime between three and four – can't you be a bit more accurate?'

'No, I can't.'

'Would it have been nearer three or nearer four?'

'Sometime between the two.'

'Nearer three or nearer four?'

'Nearer three. Just after three.'

'And he went straight back home, did he?'

'You had better ask him that; how should I know?'

'And where is he now?'

The woman looked surprised. 'At home, I suppose,' she said.

'You reckon he'll be at home with his wife?'

'If he's got one.'

'You wouldn't know that, of course, would you?'

'I don't ask my clients about their private affairs.'

C.I.D. was amused by the word *clients*. '*Clients* is good,' he said. 'I like *clients*. Well, if you do happen to hear anything of Roger Tranter's whereabouts, we want to know about it down at the station, quick. O.K.?'

The woman said nothing.

C.I.D. put his notebook away and nodded to the policewoman.

'People who withhold information in a murder enquiry can get into a lot of trouble,' he said as he rose to his feet, 'a lot of trouble.'

'I'm not withholding anything,' the woman said, 'because I don't know anything.'

'Turn it over in your mind,' C.I.D. advised, 'and you may come up with something. We'll be along again in a day or two to see you if you have.'

In the car on the way back to the station C.I.D. uttered one word. '*Clients*,' he said, and burst out laughing.

Mollie Tranter was glad to get out of the shop. There was nothing explicit, of course. Nothing openly stated. The words weren't used. She didn't think they would be. She knew enough about village life not to expect words. But the atmosphere was there. As it had been ever since Matton's body had been found in the hut. There were little sidelong glances as though people were hoping to catch her unawares and see some fleeting expression on her face which would give her away. And there were hints and cleverly veiled allusions.

Well, let them glance, she thought, let them drop their hints and fish with their clever allusions, they would get nothing out of her. But she was scared. Mortally scared. She would dearly have liked, what she knew she hadn't got in the village, someone she could trust, someone to talk things over with. On her way back to Lodge Cottage she passed the Cobalt Arms. She wanted to go in to get a bottle of sherry; there was no drink left in the cottage and she felt the need of some badly; but she kept on her way. Going into the Arms meant meeting people, maybe having to talk to people. She felt she couldn't face that. The *atmosphere* would be there, just as it had been in the shop. She wanted to get back to the cottage and shut herself away from it all.

The unpleasant things had invaded the cottage, of course. P.C. West had come first and shortly after him some of his superiors from the county town.

She had told them nothing, or as near nothing as was possible. Nothing that mattered, anyway. She was scared, dead scared, but she tried to keep her head. She kept reminding herself that none of them *knew* anything. Only one person *knew* about herself and Frederick Matton – the little stranger who had been staying at the Arms. And perhaps he only thought he knew, perhaps she had been able to put him off. Thank God he had gone, she thought, but where had he gone to? And had he said anything to anybody before he left the Arms? One moment she never wanted to see him again, the next she felt it would be a relief to get in touch with him and get some reassuring answers out of him. At least he would be somebody to talk to.

The front-door bell sounded and she thought, *Christ, it's that damned West again.*

But it wasn't P.C. West, it was the tall fellow staying at the Arms. The last time Mollie Tranter had encountered Hooky she had done her best to avoid him; now, seeing him on her doorstep, looking unmistakably amiable and friendly, she hardly knew what to do.

His first words went a long way towards deciding her.

'I've been visiting your friend Mr Furlong – '

'The little fellow as was at the Arms?' she replied slowly. 'I don't know as he is any particular friend of mine.'

'Well, he sent you his regards and all sorts of messages.'

'Messages?'

Hooky affected a shiver. 'A fresh wind today,' he suggested. 'Nippy.'

Mrs Tranter took a step backwards and said, 'Come inside.'

Inside the front room of the cottage Hooky expressed his approval of it. 'Jolly snug little place you've got here,' he said, 'just suits you and your husband I should think.' He produced the parcel he was carrying and unwrapped it. He put the bottle on a small side table. The woman eyed it in silent thanksgiving.

'As we haven't seen you in the Arms lately,' Hooky said, 'I thought you might be running short of sherry. Can you rustle up a couple of glasses?'

The glasses came from a cupboard in the corner of the room; Hooky filled them and smiled. 'Here's luck, then,' he said, 'we shall probably all need it.'

A really sweet sherry was an abomination on Hooky Hefferman's palate, but no one would have guessed it from the way he smacked his lips and exclaimed in hearty tones, 'Well, that's better, then.'

'You said *messages*,' Mollie Tranter reminded him. 'What messages did Mr Furlong send?'

'Oh, the usual sort of thing. I think the little man was rather taken by you – very understandably, if I may say so,' Hooky answered gallantly.

The woman responded automatically with a faint smile, but she didn't really feel much like smiling. 'Is he coming back here?' she asked.

Hooky shook his head. 'Shouldn't think so. I think he did all he wanted to.'

'Did all he wanted to? What was that?'

'Apparently he had some business with Sir Frederick Matton.'

'I thought he was bird-watching.'

'He *said* he was. Maybe it was something of a hobby of his. It was an excuse to take him up into the woods anyway.'

Mollie Tranter was silent for a moment, then she asked, 'What did you mean just now about us all needing luck?'

Hooky smiled at her and said, 'Life gets complicated at times. We all do it, you know; get ourselves into a jam, I mean. Lord, the idiocies I've let myself in for in my time and the luck I've needed to get out of them.'

The woman studied him, considering. 'And did you have the luck?' she asked at length.

'I managed; as the saying goes, the devil looks after his own.'

'I don't know as there is anything particularly devilish about it,' Mollie Tranter said slowly.

'Neither do I,' Hooky agreed, 'neither do I. But it has gone sour on you, hasn't it? A man has been shot and rather naturally people are asking who did it.'

'West, and the others, have been asking me.'

'And they'll go on asking you; once that lot get inquisitive about a thing they have a habit of sticking at it.'

'Like god-damned dogs on a scent they are,' the woman said bitterly. 'Roger told me about that. You fall foul of the law, he said, and, Christ, they don't give you a chance.'

'Where is Roger, by the way?'

'I don't know where he is, and that's the truth.'

Hooky was watching the woman's face as she said this; after a moment's pause he nodded and said, 'I believe you.'

'I wish the others did.'

'Do you think your husband killed Matton?'

She caught his eye and looked away again quickly. 'How do I know who killed him?' she mumbled.

'How indeed?' Hooky answered lightly. 'What everyone is curious about is what was Matton doing in the hut.'

'It's on his land, isn't it? I suppose he can go into it if

he wants. He might have been up there blackberrying.'

'Or like the couple who found him, after a bit of slap and tickle.'

Mollie Tranter held out her glass to be replenished with the sweet sherry and said, 'They've got it in for Roger because he has been inside.'

'They do tend to go after the old customers.'

'Ah, you can joke about it. Maybe you don't know what prison does to a man. It doesn't cure them of being villains, I can tell you that. And there are just as big villains outside. Roger always says so. The big man in the City. He even said it about Matton himself; and Mr Donaldson the accountant; all villains, he often said.'

'Is Donaldson a villain?'

'The way Roger talks we all are more or less. Men go for what they want, that's my experience. Donaldson's like the rest of you, I expect, out for number one.'

'Did he ever call here?'

'Of course he did. A number of times; if he had been up at the house and there was a message for Roger from Sir Frederick.'

'Did he call here on Tuesday afternoon?'

'No, he didn't, mister. So you are being a bit too clever, aren't you? It was Tuesday morning, if you want to know.'

'With a message for your husband?'

'Are you trying to get Roger into trouble? Christ, you're as bad as West and all the rest of them.'

Hooky studied the strong, characterful face for a second or two in silence. Whichever way the game went there was something about this woman that he had to admire; he felt that if the dice had fallen another way she might easily have come to fame. He was by no means certain, even now, that she wouldn't make the headlines; he was by no means certain who it was that he was trying to get into trouble.

CHAPTER THIRTEEN

You can't help wondering

P.C. West replaced the telephone.

'The Inspector again?' his wife asked.

'Who else? Anyone would think there were forty-eight hours in the day the amount of work they expect me to get through.'

'Have they found anything?'

'Yes, they have. They've found something more for me to do. It's Sweeting Bog now. *We don't think he's anywhere local*, the Inspector said, *but we've got to make sure. So you'd better take a damned good look at Sweeting Bog this morning and let me know the result when you get back*.'

'You'll be late for your dinner then?'

'I'll be late for dinner all right, when am I anything else? To take what the Inspector calls a damned good look at the Bog you want four men and a couple of days.'

'I'll keep something in the oven. That shepherd's pie will warm up nicely.'

The policeman nodded. He liked shepherd's pie. 'I'll get back as soon as I can,' he promised. 'It's a waste of time anyway.'

'You don't think he's in the Bog then?'

'I'm sure he isn't. Roger Tranter would have more sense. It's not his style anyway. He's used to going here, there and everwhere with Matton on all sorts of journeys. They don't want to send the local man to Sweeting Bog, they want to get on to Interpol.'

'I suppose they've got to do both,' his wife ventured to suggest.

'Well, maybe they have,' West agreed. 'They've got to cover everything.'

'Will they be asking that nice man staying at the Arms to help?'

'They will *not*. What use is a Private Investigator anyway? What does he investigate and who employs him? Some old lady who loses her cat, I suppose. He hasn't got the facilities, the apparatus. I've always got the Inspector behind me.'

Ethel West couldn't help recalling her husband's frequently expressed opinion of the Inspector and of higher police authority generally; but she had a woman's wisdom; she refrained from referring to it.

'And after the shepherd's pie I've a nice piece of that Dutch cheese as you're so fond of,' she said.

'I'll be back as soon as I've done the job,' the policeman promised again.

His wife saw him to the door. 'I suppose they'll find him in the end,' she said.

'Oh, we'll find him in the end right enough.'

'But, of course, we're not sure he did it, are we?'

The policeman laughed. 'Aren't we?' he said.

Sweeting had never figured in the national press before; now it was getting almost daily mention and looked as though it might achieve the headlines at any moment.

The first thing that every Sweetingite looked for each morning in his *Mail, Express, Sun* or *Mirror* was any reference to what was known as the murder in the hut. The world currencies might be in chaos; the outbreak of large-scale war in the Middle East might be imminent; a new type of nuclear bomb with more than usual horrifying potentialities might have been invented – all these minor matters were hastily skipped over in the search for a mention of the village and of the hunt for Roger Tranter.

'I hate it,' Martha Old said.

The time was just after half past ten, which meant that your free-born Englishman, who was prepared on suitable occasions to state vociferously, even if completely out of tune, that he would never, never, never be a slave, was now allowed to have a drink.

Hooky was doing that very thing; and since no other customer had yet come into the Arms Martha Old had ventured to join him in the bar where the inescapable topic was being discussed by Hooky, her husband and herself.

'It's meat and drink to Harry West,' Old said. 'Of course he grumbles all the time – too much to do and he does it all himself whilst the others just sit on their backsides, and so on; but the truth is he's enjoying himself. Well, you can understand it, can't you? Remember how he went on about Colorado beetles when he came in here with that poster? It must be a relief to get away from Colorado beetles and boys scrumping and have something real to do for a change.'

'If I was a policeman,' Mrs Old said, 'I'd a lot sooner have scrumping boys to deal with than a murder.'

'Well, no one likes a murder exactly,' her husband allowed, 'of course they don't. But the point is we've got one. Like it or not. And so we've got to find who did it. We've got a chase on; it's like a hunt.'

'That's exactly why I hate it,' Martha Old reiterated. 'I hate hunting.'

'Oh dear, dear, dear.' Charles Old was shocked. He had the greatest admiration for his wife whom he truly regarded as the salt of the earth. But every now and again he didn't want salt with his food. 'Hunting's part of the countryside,' he said. 'Always has been. You won't see a finer sight than the pink coats and the hounds and the whole meet on the lawn in front of the big house – like we used to have at the Hall, Mr Hefferman, and my word to see your aunt riding side-saddle! She looked magnificent; you knew what a lady was when you saw her.'

'I'll bet she put the wind up the fox,' Hooky said.

'If ever a fox came into our garden here,' Martha Old declared, 'and the hunt after it I'd send them packing, Master and all, I can tell you. All those people and a whole lot of dogs after one little animal; and not content with that, during the night someone has been round and stopped up the earth so that the poor creature has nowhere to hide. Then they tell you what good sport it all is!'

'The world ought to be run by women,' Hooky said.

'Well, they might make a good job of some things,' Old allowed, 'but what about justice? If there isn't such a thing we may as well all throw our hands in. A man has been killed and someone has done it; and it's up to the community to find out who that someone is.'

'I suppose so,' his wife sighed, 'only I wish the papers wouldn't make such a meal of it, they seem to gloat over it.'

'You mustn't rob the glorious British Press of its fair game,' Hooky said. 'A man on the run; the widow of some poor devil killed in an accident and not yet cold; a woman whose two children have just been burnt to death – if the Press boys aren't allowed to wring the last drop of sentiment out of people like this how are the poor chaps going to earn their two hundred a week?'

'The only thing I really enjoy in the paper is the *What's in Your Stars* column,' Martha Old said, 'and I don't mind what it says there because I know it isn't true.'

'Precisely why I read the Parliamentary reports,' Hooky told her. 'Hansard and Gretel. Great stuff.'

Donaldson came into the bar and the talk instantly and inevitably swung back to the only topic the village was really interested in. When genuine information is hard to come by crumbs are welcome; and since the accountant was part of the dead man's firm it was assumed that he must have access to some store of inside knowledge.

It was an assumption against which he now made vigorous disclaimer. He fended off enquiries with a sort of humorous irritation. 'I don't know any more than anybody else, I'm completely in the dark.'

'You haven't heard anything of Tranter's whereabouts?' Hooky enquired.

'Still full of curiosity, are you?' Donaldson said with a touch of sharpness in his voice. 'Well, I've just told you, I don't know any more than anybody else.'

'Do you reckon as Roger Tranter did it?' Old asked the blunt question.

The accountant ordered his drink and appeared to be considering whilst it was served to him; finally he said, 'I refuse to answer that question. Because I don't think it's a fair one. After all, this is England, isn't it? Not a police state. Roger Tranter isn't even in court yet. He hasn't been charged with anything yet. I don't think we ought to start saying whether he's guilty or not until he's actually on trial.'

'I wish everyone thought like that,' Martha Old said.

'Still, you must admit it looks a bit funny his going off into the blue all of a sudden,' Old persisted.

Donaldson laughed. A little, hard, dry sound that didn't have much mirth about it. A laugh which Hooky, who often judged men by their laughter, didn't much like. Nor did he like the owner of the laugh much; but he listened with interest to what the man was saying and he had to admit the fairness of a lot of it.

'Anyone who worked for Matton soon got used to funny things. And to things happening in a hurry. I've known him before now send Tranter off at a moment's notice with some personal message to someone hundreds of miles away. Still, since you ask me, yes, things do look a bit funny at the moment, I agree. And, of course, when a man has got a record, like Roger Tranter has, you can't help wondering, can you?'

'What I can't help wondering,' Hooky said, 'is why Matton was in the hut at all.'

'It's in the woods,' Donaldson offered in explanation. '*His* woods, after all. Drage says Sir Frederick often went for an afternoon walk up there.'

'Did you see Drage that afternoon?'

'Of course I did. If you are still so full of curiosity about other people's business, Drage can satisfy it for you. He'll tell you I was at Leys at half past three. Expecting to see Sir Frederick. Only of course he wasn't there. He was up in the woods. Possibly he was walking by the hut and heard noises of somebody inside and looked in to see who it was.'

'And who was it?' Hooky asked.

Donaldson laughed again. 'Some people are never satisfied, are they?' he said. 'How do I know who it was? A tramp, maybe; and there's a scuffle; What the hell are you doing in here? Matton asks – he's got a quick temper. It gets out of hand and there you are.'

'A tramp!' Hooky exclaimed. 'I haven't seen a real, live, genuine, hole-in-the-toe-of-his-socks tramp for years. Social security has abolished tramps. And, anyway, a tramp carrying a gun?'

'Unlikely,' Donaldson admitted. 'Of course, Matton might have gone up there expecting to meet someone.'

'And who would that someone be?'

'I dare say there are people in the village who could make a better guess at that than I can,' the accountant said, 'and, in any case, I only put it forward as a suggestion. We've got to allow for every possibility, haven't we? But, when you come to think of it, that hut up in the woods would be a very convenient place for a meeting, an assignation, wouldn't it?'

Twenty minutes later Hooky was walking through the village, the conversation in the Arms still fresh in his mind. *Powerful things, words*, he thought; *assignation; there's a nasty word for you; hissed by a clever prosecuting counsel 'assignation' is halfway to condemning any man.*

As he passed the village shop he saw two women outside it engaged in voluble conversation; a little further on the milkman, bottle in hand, was earnestly discussing something with a housewife. No prizes for guessing what they are all talking about, Hooky thought; and he wished it had been otherwise, the innocence seemed to have gone out of the place.

He was glad to reach the cricket ground where he was alone except for the ancient who seemed to be a permanent fixture on the wooden bench by the pavilion. The ancient was delighted to have someone to talk to, particularly an ignorant stranger unversed in Sweeting lore and stories; he hailed Hooky instantly.

'Know why they kept it up there?' he demanded.

'Kept what up?'

The old man's opinion of the low intelligence of all non-Sweetingites was confirmed. 'Why, *that* of course,' he answered sharply, pointing to the score-board. 'What do you think I'm talking about?'

Hooky considered the figures on the board, 87—9—0.

'I suppose they forgot to take it down,' he ventured.

'Ah well, that just shows how much you don't know, doesn't it?' the Sweetingite pointed out with great satisfaction. 'Nobody forgot nothing. That's kept up on purpose, that is. That was in the last match of the season, that was. Against Briarly. We were batting. It was last man in and that meant Fred Oakes. Fred worked on the Leys farm. A big chap. Liked his beer. Ten pints in an evening was nothing to him. And he liked his cricket too. But it was one thing or t'other with Fred, he was as likely to get out first ball as he was to score twenty in an over. So there he was last man in and only a few wanted to win. Ten or twelve, I forget exactly. Fred hits the ball, not a proper clout but there were runs in it. *Come on,* he shouts, and they ran two, as fast as they could. Too fast for Fred. When he got back to his end down he went in a heap on the ground. Purple in his face; his heart gone. *"Well,"* he said, *"it's been a good game,"* and those were the very last words he spoke. The whole village turned out for his funeral and the club sent a wreath. I wonder these florist people don't all retire and go and live in Spain the prices they charge. The club secretary said, *Let's keep the score up on the board till next season; it's the last thing old Fred saw and it'll remind us of him.*'

Hooky was moved by the simple story. 'What a splendid memorial,' he said. 'It's what ought to have been done at Granchester; they ought to have left the church clock permanently at ten to three.'

'What are you talking about now?' the ancient asked suspiciously.

'I was thinking of a chap called Rupert Brooke.'

'Who did he play for?'

'The Romantics, I suppose.'

'Never heard of 'em. One of your bits and pieces sides, I shouldn't wonder.'

'I don't think they would cut much ice these days,' Hooky

agreed sadly. 'This chap Oakes worked on the Leys farm, you say?'

'Ever since he was a lad. Do anything. Cowman; drive the tractor; hedging; a bit of thatching when they wanted it; get the land girl in trouble – anything. And I can tell you one thing, mister, Fred wouldn't be wearing no mourning today. He couldn't abide Matton. *Someone will kill that bugger one day*, he used to say.'

'How right he was,' Hooky said. 'But, of course, the question is who?'

'Does it matter?'

The question took Hooky slightly aback. 'When anybody gets killed,' he said, 'it's generally thought to be a good idea to find out who did it.'

'Waffle,' the ancient proclaimed. 'Blah-blah-blah stuff. In the last twenty-four hours a few hundred people died of starvation in India alone; by this time tomorrow there'll be another few hundred gone. Are you fussing about them, mister? I'm not. I don't give a damn. How many men are there in England round about the eighty mark? Don't ask me how old I am because I shan't tell you. You can lay odds that four out of ten of them have killed men in their day. Nineteen-fourteen to nineteen-eighteen. Heroes in khaki. Some heroes. Most of us wetting our breeches through fear half the time. We got medals for killing them. The parsons stood up in the pulpit and told us what a good job we were doing killing Jerries. Who cared about all that? Now, if one single man is found dead (and, dammit, we've all got to come to it sometime) God Almighty, what a fuss. Half a dozen policemen on the job; a thing called an "incident headquarters" set up; photographs and measurements; all the papers on about it; TV, radio, the lot.'

'I still think it's a good idea to run the chap to earth,' Hooky persisted.

The ancient shook his head. 'Not worth it,' he pronounced. 'Not these days. When a man got hanged for murder there was some real excitement in it. There was fun in murder trials then. Everyone enjoyed it. When the judge put on the black cap the public gallery really felt they were getting their money's worth. But nowadays – ' He shrugged his shoulders. 'Suppose they catch Roger Tranter, what does it really amount to? There's no real drama in it, is there?'

'So you reckon Tranter did it?'

'Don't go putting words in my mouth, mister. That's a proper foreigner's trick that is. We aren't all simpletons at Sweeting, you know. There's plenty of folk round here know how many beans make five. I never said Tranter did it. Mind you, he might have done. It depends on what Matton had been up to. Every man jack of us carries his bit of fun around with him between his legs, and one way and another it gets us all into a lot of trouble. But then again it might not have been like that at all. Matton was in big business, and Roger Tranter was only the chauffeur, he had nothing to do with big business. But even if you look at it that way you've still got to explain why he went off all of a sudden, haven't you?'

'Truth is a bashful goddess and no man knows at what altar she may be found.'

'Who said that?' the ancient asked suspiciously.

'Mr Chu-Ling. A Chinese gentleman.'

'The sort of thing you would expect a Chink to say,' the Sweetingite declared. 'The Chinese never played a game of cricket in their lives.'

When he was well beyond the cricket field on the road which, had he continued on it, would have taken him in a wide loop right round the village Hooky fell in with the boy Dent.

Charlie Dent was carrying a jam-jar in which a goldfish swam restrictively.

'Hallo,' Hooky greeted him. 'Just got him, have you?'

'Don't be daft, mister,' Charlie begged. 'I've had him nearly two years. Freddie he's called.'

Hooky laughed. 'And does he know his name?' he asked.

'Of course he knows his name. Same as you do. People think fish are silly, but they aren't. It's people as are silly.'

'Maybe you've got something there,' Hooky allowed.

'And now I'm selling him. Do you want to buy him, mister? A quid to you. I bet you can afford it.'

'Thanks for the compliment,' Hooky said, 'but what would I do with a goldfish? And why do you want to sell Freddie, anyway?'

'I never said as I want to sell him. I don't want to sell him; but I've got to sell him if I'm going to get four pounds twenty-five.'

'And you want four pounds twenty-five, do you?'

'Of course I want four pounds twenty-five. To get my skateboard mended. They'll do it for me up at the garage, but it will cost four twenty-five.'

'Won't your father give you the money?'

'The only thing my dad will give me is a leathering. Fat-arse West has put my dad against me for good, he keeps telling him what a nuisance I am and my dad reckons if I haven't got any money I can't get into trouble, so he keeps me short. If you ask me, the police ought to be abolished; is that right what they say in the village that you're a Private Eye, mister?'

'I expect they say a lot of things in the village.'

Charlie Dent viewed Hooky critically; it was evident that the stranger didn't come up to what the boy thought a Private Eye should look like.

'Well, if you are a Private Eye,' he said, 'I bet you don't half see some exciting things. Is it like it is on the telly?'

'Not a great deal.'

'Have you got a gun?'

'I left it in my other suit.'

'I'll bet. What will you do if you catch Roger Tranter?'

'I'm not after Roger Tranter.'

'Westy is, isn't he?'

'P.C. West is a conscientious officer who knows what his duty is and will carry it out.'

'Don't make me laugh, mister. Old Fat-arse wouldn't catch a tortoise in a blind alley. Besides, he doesn't know everything, does he?'

'No one knows everything.'

Charlie Dent smiled and began to whistle jauntily. Inspiration came to Hooky. He brought out his wallet and extracted a five-pound note. He dangled the piece of paper in the air. It looked tempting.

'How about getting that skateboard of yours fixed,' Hooky suggested.

The boy extended his hand, and the bait was moved a little further out of reach.

'What is it you know that West doesn't?' Hooky asked.

'I was up in Silverman's that afternoon. I ought not to have been; I ought to have been in school. "If I hear of you dodging school again," my dad said, "I'll give you the best beating you've ever had." So of course I haven't told anyone.'

'But that Tuesday afternoon you were in Silverman's Wood, near the hut?'

'Just at the back of it. And I saw this chap come out.'

'You saw Roger Tranter come out of the hut?'

'Not Roger Tranter, mister; Matton's other man, the one who comes to see him at Leys every now and again.'

'The accountant, Donaldson?'

'That's the one, mister.'

The five-pound note changed hands.

CHAPTER FOURTEEN

Truncated trochaic octometers

Herbert Aston looked round the room a little guiltily. Its untidiness had reached a pitch which even he found noticeable. The tutorial was due in a few minutes, and it occurred to him that Mrs Andrews wouldn't think much of the state the place was in; an unreasonable view to take of things, he considered, because, after all, what did this female fetish about tidiness amount to? It consisted essentially in picking things up from one place, where they were doing no harm, anyway, and moving them somewhere else where, the odds were, you would never be able to find them. Unreasonable it might be but that was the way, the Professor realised, that the feminine mind worked and it was up to him as a man of the world (a role he now fancied himself in) to know about these things and to act on them.

The air was still thick with the dust of his tentative tidying up when the doorbell rang.

'Good heavens,' Dorothea cried coming into the small room. 'Whatever is happening? What a frightful dust.'

'I was tidying up a bit,' the Professor said, 'in preparation for your visit, I may point out,' he added with a slight note of asperity in his voice.

Dorothea laughed. 'That was nice of you, Professor,' she said. 'May I suggest that it would be a good thing to have a window open?'

'You may make the suggestion,' Herbert Aston replied tartly, 'but it is not one that I shall implement. Of all the fallacies that the human mind deludes itself with, the one about the supposedly beneficial value of fresh air is one of the most pernicious. So-called fresh air isn't good for anybody, it's a dangerous germ-laden commodity.'

Dorothea laughed again. 'I'm sure you know best,' she said. 'We'll just let the dust settle.'

'If I hadn't moved things there wouldn't be any dust,' Aston pointed out, 'and I wouldn't have moved them if you hadn't been coming.'

'So it's really all my fault?'

'It usually is the woman's fault,' the Professor said complacently. 'You remember Milton's magnificent opening to *Paradise Lost*: *of man's first disobedience* and so on. All that was the woman's fault, wasn't it?'

'Professor,' Dorothea told him in mock severity, 'you are a male chauvinist – but nothing would induce me to complete the phrase.'

Herbert Aston, in his innocence, didn't know the completion of the phrase so he wasn't worried. 'Now then,' he began, '*Locksley Hall*. You've been studying it, haven't you? Truncated trochaic octometers. Aren't those magnificent words? Like banners flying.'

Dorothea smiled at his enthusiasm; but Tennyson's truncated octometers would have to wait a bit.

'Before we get on to Locksley Hall,' she said, 'won't you tell me something about the châteaux of the Loire?'

'Ah – the châteaux of the Loire.' The Professor had almost forgotten having said anything about the châteaux of the Loire and the effort he now had to make to call the matter to mind was obvious.

Watching him Dorothea smiled gently . . . Dear little man, she thought; all men are poor liars and this one is fundamentally so honest that he is a very poor liar indeed . . . he really needs somebody to look after him; somebody to keep the place dusted and open the windows occasionally; and it isn't as though he's *old*; he's in vigorous middle age; surely there ought to be *somebody* . . . The possibility even occurred to her that that somebody might turn out to be herself . . . *Professor and Widowed Undergraduate to Wed*, she could see the headlines already and could imagine the stir they would make in the University . . .

' – yes, the châteaux of the Loire,' she repeated remorselessly.

Herbert Aston reached for his pipe. Dorothea waited, wondering in silent amusement what fabrication his fertile mind would produce this time.

'Filling a pipe properly is a very tricky business,' the Professor said.

'I've noticed that you spend a lot of time doing it,' Dorothea answered.

'In a way it's akin to making a bonfire, there's a definite art in it.'

'Were there any bonfires at the châteaux?'

The Professor gave careful attention to tamping down the tobacco in the bowl of his beloved pipe before replying. 'As a matter of fact I didn't go to the châteaux of the Loire at all.'

'No; instead you went to a place called Sweeting. The Cobalt Arms, wasn't it? Where you made the acquaintance of an engaging creature called Hefferman.'

The description of Hooky amused Herbert Aston. 'An engaging creature,' he repeated, 'that's just what he is. Academically negligible, no doubt; but alpha plus in the business of living. What I don't understand is how you and he came to know one another.'

'A little bit of detective work on the engaging creature's part. You lent him my copy of *Double Fault* and there was a éticket for the S.S.C.A. raffle in it.'

'Ah well, that explains that. It is always so much more satisfactory to the mind when the *reason* for anything becomes apparent. Now shall we turn to *Locksley Hall* – '

'Confound *Locksley Hall.*'

The Professor looked up in astonishment.

'I'm sorry, Herbert, to have startled you,' Dorothea went on, 'and you must allow me for once to address you by your Christian name. Of course I am only too content in normal circumstances for the relationship between us to be that of tutor and pupil. But, after all, I am a widow with a teenage daughter; you and I are both adults; and really these are hardly normal circumstances, are they? Even with your bland indifference to practical things, Herbert, you must admit what you told me about your brother and sister-in-law; and then your going off to this Sweeting place under an assumed name; and then on top of that Sir Frederick Matton being found dead – even you must admit that all this adds up to something that can hardly be called normal.'

'Life is a very strange affair,' the Professor said dreamily. 'It would be very interesting to have some dependable definition of what the normal really is.'

Dorothea shook her head vigorously. 'Sorry,' she told him, 'but I have no intention of letting you escape down nebulous philosophical avenues. We'll have a lovely discussion about philosophical definitives and truncated trochaic octometers later. At the moment it's Sweeting and the Cobalt Arms and what you were doing there.'

'I admire your tenacity of purpose, Dorothea,' the Professor answered, 'just as, if you will allow me to say it, I have come to admire many things about you in the course of our tutorials together – oh dear – now who the devil can that be?'

In view of the turn the conversation was taking Dorothea was as annoyed as he was at the interrupting doorbell.

'Tell whoever it is that you're busy,' she advised.

Whether the Professor did in fact try to fob off his caller with a statement about being busy Dorothea didn't know; the conversation in the hall was muffled and indistinct. But even if fobbing off was attempted it obviously wasn't successful, for when Herbert Aston came back into the room he was followed by Hooky Hefferman.

'The engaging creature,' the Professor said drily. 'He seemed apt to the situation so I invited him in.'

The engaging creature and Dorothea Andrews smiled at one another and inspiration seized Dorothea.

'Herbert,' she said sharply, 'I've a feeling that this is an occasion for a drink. You must have a bottle of something somewhere.'

One of the several bookcases in the room had a cupboard

in its lower part. Rummaging a little uncertainly in this cupboard, Aston produced a bottle and three glasses.

'Sercial,' he said, 'a wine I can heartily recommend. I'm afraid the glasses may be a trifle dusty.'

'A little dust never hurt anybody,' Hooky declared cheerfully.

'Precisely what I was pointing out to Mrs Andrews some time back,' the Professor said, 'but you know what women are!'

'Only too well.'

Dorothea smiled sweetly at the two males. 'Shall we postpone a discussion of Mr Hefferman's love life,' she suggested, 'and get on with the matter in hand. Shall I pour the drinks out, Herbert? What did you call it? Sercial?'

'Good job it isn't sweet sherry,' Hooky said. 'You remember the woman who drank sweet sherry, Prof.?'

Aston winced at the abbreviation, and Dorothea, pouring out, laughed. 'It sounds like the title of a short story,' she said. '*The Woman Who Drank Sweet Sherry* – do tell me about her.'

'I think she was a bit of a *femme fatale*,' Hooky said, 'and I'm not sure the Prof. didn't have a narrow escape; he seemed to me to be inclined to roll an eye at the lady.'

'May we get one thing settled,' Herbert Aston said in his sharpest scholastic tones. 'This vulgar abbreviation of the dignified title Professor which you persist in using – kindly drop it. I find it highly objectionable. My name is Herbert Aston. For family reasons, which I don't propose to go into, I was christened Herbert Eugene Napoleon Aston; but Herbert will do. I am delighted to say that Mrs Andrews, Dorothea, has taken to calling me by that name, and I have no objection to your doing so as well.'

Dorothea caught Hooky's eye, and each knew how difficult the other was finding it not to burst into laughter.

Dorothea composed her features and asked with mock seriousness, 'Herbert, did you really have an affair with someone in Sweeting?'

The Professor vouchsafed the silly matter a sardonic smile.

'Far be it from me to suggest that Mr Hefferman doesn't always tell the truth,' he said, 'let me say instead that he is a great performer in the picaresque vein.'

Dorothea could contain herself no longer. *What a perfectly splendid little man Herbert is,* she thought. She burst out laughing and said, 'I must say that seems to me to be an admirable description of you, Mr Hefferman.'

'Hooky – since we seem to have come down to personalities.'

Dorothea beamed at him. 'Yes, that suits you, too,' she said. 'Well, do go on Hooky and tell me more about the lady who liked sweet sherry.'

'The lady with the unfortunate taste in sherry,' Hooky said 'was called Mollie. Mollie Tranter. A good-looker in her way. A bit of the gypsy about her, I shouldn't wonder. You noticed it in the way she walked. A swing and swagger about it. I doubt if women realise how badly most of them walk and how seductively attractive a good style of walking can be.'

Herbert Aston nodded his enthusiastic agreement with all this.

> 'Whenas in silks my Julia goes (he quoted)
> Then, then (methinks) how sweetly flows
> That liquefaction of her clothes.
> Next, when I cast mine eyes and see
> That brave vibration each way free;
> Oh how that glittering taketh me!'

Dorothea was so enchanted by the aptness of the quotation that she actually applauded softly. 'Isn't he marvellous, Hooky?' she demanded. 'He always knows exactly the right thing to say. No wonder he got on well with Mollie – what's her name.'

'Tranter. Mollie Tranter. Wife of Sir Frederick Matton's chauffeur. And that, of course, opens up the plot, doesn't it, Herbert?'

'I suppose so,' the Professor said. 'As a rational being I must say I find it very disappointing that practically every single plot, either in fiction or reality, hinges on what I may perhaps be allowed to call sub-navel activity.'

'The comic-farce of life runs on ball-bearing lines,' Hooky said solemnly.

'It would appear to,' Aston agreed. 'No doubt the arrangement suits some people. I expect it suited Matton. At any rate, as you know, I happened to see him come out of the hut up in the woods a minute or two after the lady we are talking about, Mollie Tranter, had walked away from it. Of course at the time I didn't know who either of them was.'

'But when you found out you very sensibly put the bite on Matton and squeezed five thousand pounds out of him.'

'Your language seems to be sadly affected by what I believe people refer to as the box; but, though stereotyped in expression, in essence what you say is right.'

'You got five thousand pounds out of Sir Frederick Matton?' Dorothea cried. 'Oh, well done!'

So Don Quixote tilted at his windmill and for once the windmill got the worst of it, Hooky thought; well, the fools of this world had to win sometimes and on the whole it was rather refreshing when they did.

'What took place between Sir Frederick Matton and myself,' the Professor said, 'was purely a matter of conscience – '

'I doubt if Matton had much of that commodity,' Hooky put in; 'say a matter of your conscience and his convenience.'

Aston was visibly annoyed by the interruption and watching him Dorothea had difficulty in suppressing a smile; she could almost hear the words '*Quiet at the back of the class*.'

'It's true that by accident I happened to learn something of the man's private life,' Aston continued, 'but I am a great believer in privacy. Matton's private life was his own concern and nobody else's – '

'Really, you men are quite insufferable,' Dorothea cried. 'Even the nicest of you. *Nobody else's?* What about the chauffeur's wife and the chauffeur himself? Wasn't what Matton got up to some concern of theirs? All this talk about believing in privacy means that you want to be free to misbehave in the same way yourselves when it suits you. No wonder Roger Tranter killed Matton.'

'I'm not at all sure that he did,' Hooky said.

'Well, if his wife did it I'm almost inclined to say good luck to her. People who break homes and marriages deserve everything they get.'

'If we get what we deserve who should escape whipping?' Aston said. 'Shakespeare comes up with something for every need; but I wouldn't like to think it was the woman.'

'I'm prepared to believe that she was capable of it,' Hooky said. 'She struck me as being a pretty tough baby – maybe she had to be, being married to Roger Tranter; but I doubt if she did the shooting.'

'And are you going to tell us who did do it?' Dorothea asked with a slight suggestion of sarcasm in her voice.

Hooky grinned at her and said, 'No, I'm not. Not for certain. And I doubt if anyone will ever be able to tell us for certain, even when the case comes to court. Very few murder cases are settled on certainties. Circumstantial evidence isn't certain by the nature of it; and that's what ninety-nine out of a hundred murder cases are decided on. But a clever prosecuting counsel can usually put forward a pretty convincing-sounding theory.'

And you've got a theory?'

'I'm a *why* man, not a *how* man,' Hooky explained. 'The *how* men run round with magnifying glasses and cameras and tracker dogs and all the rest of it. Very clever and often enough very effective. Up to a point. But in a way it's the wrong end, isn't it? Things don't start there. Things start in a man's mind. When I see a man doing something a bit out of the ordinary I want to know why.

'If a man lies I want to know why.

'Now the Prof. here – sorry, Herbert here – lied about his name when he booked in at the Cobalt Arms. And that's entirely understandable, that was his incurable romanticism.'

'My what?' asked the Professor. Like many people who live at one remove from reality he liked to think of himself as eminently practical.

'If that university of yours has an Amateur Dramatic Society you make haste to join it,' Hooky advised him. 'You'd be a wow. You saw yourself cast for the part of Richard Furlong, bird-watcher and righter of wrongs, and you gave a jolly good performance in it. You wanted a stage name. So we understand why you should tell fibs about who you were. But why should Donaldson lie? That was what I wondered.'

'Did he lie?' Dorothea asked.

'Pretty consistently. About *time* to start with and accountants have an obsession about time. I suppose it comes from worrying so much about figures. And, mind you, occasionally the exact time matters a hell of a lot. If a man's due to be hanged at nine a.m. sharp there's quite a difference between 8.59 and 9.01. Donaldson went out of his way to impress on us all – simple, rustic innocents that we were in his eyes – that he didn't get to the village until a few minutes before three-thirty when, according to him, he had an appointment to see Matton.

'The first thing to say about that is that it seems very doubtful whether he did in fact have any such appointment. It's impossible to prove that he didn't; but it is legitimate to have doubts about it. In my opinion Drage would make a very good witness in the box and he is certainly emphatic that Matton always warned him if a visitor, particularly a business visitor, was expected; and no such warning of Donaldson's visit had been given. Naturally Donaldson didn't see Matton when he called at Leys at three-thirty sharp, because Matton was then lying in the hut in Silverman's Wood with a hole blown through his head.

'I suggest to you, members of the jury – this is how these lawyer types go on,' Hooky explained with a grin, 'I suggest to you that at three-thirty sharp, when he called at the house with a story about an appointment, Donaldson knew perfectly well where Matton was and the condition he was in. Or if he didn't we shall want an explanation of what he was doing in the village long before three-thirty on the afternoon of that day and why he lied about being there.'

'How do we know that he was in the village long before three-thirty?' Dorothea asked. 'Who saw him?'

'I, said the fly, with my little eye,' Hooky answered. 'I had been listening to some fascinating cricketing reminiscences from a venerable villager who ought to be snapped up by the radio people, he's a lot more human than Arlott and less prompous than Swanton; when I left him I walked on through the churchyard intending to fetch a circle round the village. Immediately beyond the churchyard there's a sunken lane which doesn't seem to lead anywhere in particular and in the lane there was a car parked. Which struck me at the time as being a shade odd. By and large the English don't worship God much these days and they certainly don't do it at a quarter to twelve on a weekday; besides which the church was very sensibly shut. As the Scripture has it, this is my house and the gates of it shall not be open by day or by night in case vandals get in and play merry hell with everything.'

'I've a feeling that that quotation is not entirely accurate,' the Professor said.

Hooky said he hoped that it wasn't. 'Accuracy,' he pointed out, 'is the small end of the telescope. Truth comes out of the other end.'

'Perhaps we could have your philosophic thesis some other time.' Dorothea suggested tartly. 'What about the car in the lane?'

'I didn't know whose it was at the time, of course. I simply put the odd little fact of its being there in my E.C.B.'

'Your what?'

'Earnest Consideration Box. The rag-bag of odds and ends one picks up during the day, things which may be worth having a second look at later on. When Donaldson came to the Arms that evening I saw that the car was his and I realised that he must have been in the village long before the time he was so keen to impress on us.

'Now, if he was lying (as I know he was) about the time he reached the village, and if he was lying (as seemed probable) about having an appointment to see Matton, then one of my six honest serving men put up his hand and asked a very loud and insistent *why*. The bits and pieces in the E.C.B. were beginning to look interesting.

'And another of the serving men, called Mr What, began to ask questions, too. What was Donaldson doing between a quarter past twelve when I saw his car in the sunken lane by the church and three-thirty when he turned up at Leys? I'll tell you one thing he did that morning, he called at Lodge Cottage. He may well have been doing so at the actual time I saw his car parked in the lane.'

'How do you know he called there?' Dorothea asked.

'Mollie Tranter told me he did. I doubt if she specifically meant to tell me. She had probably made up her mind the less she said about anything to anybody the better. A very wise decision, too. But it came out in the course of conversation.'

'What did Donaldson say to her when he called there?'

'I didn't ask her. But believe me, if prosecuting Counsel get her in the witness box they'll want to know. Those gentlemen with their gowns and wigs and their fat retainers and refreshers will give her a pretty rough time in court. I didn't ask her what he said; and if I had asked her she probably wouldn't have told me. But I've a theory. You have got to remember, Herbert, that apart from the two principals themselves, you were the only person who knew that they used the hut up in the woods as a place of – marvellous word, isn't it? – *assignation*.

'Knowing Roger Tranter's character and his reputation for violence you can bet your boots they were careful. Some people in the village may have suspected there was some funny business going on, but apparently Tranter himself didn't. Maybe he was too busy with his own bits of nonsense in Reading and elsewhere. But there's never been an intrigue yet in which the lover didn't have to jump out of the bedroom window eventually; you can be as careful as you know how but you get rumbled in time –'

'Which I am sure you have often found highly inconvenient,' Dorothea said.

Hooky smiled amiably at her. He liked Mrs Andrews; he wasn't going to allow an occasional asperity on her part to put him off his stroke. ' – it usually happens by accident,' he continued placidly. 'In this porticular instance you were the accident, Herbert. By chance you came to know that the two of them were using the hut, and (most important of all) you told Donaldson – '

The Professor nodded. 'True. I did. Donaldson came to see me at the Arms. I'm not quite sure why. At the time I assumed that Matton must have sent him to buy me off, or frighten me, at any rate to sound me out in some way. But subsequently, in thinking over what he said and the way he said it I'm not so sure of that. In any case, what you are saying is true; yes, I did let him know about Matton and Mrs Tranter. I suggested to him that a man who wasn't above seducing the wife of his chauffeur could hardly be regarded as a man of honour.'

'Somehow I've a feeling that Donaldson didn't rate Matton very high in the honour stakes anyway. And if there wasn't any love lost between them what he learnt from you, Herbert, would have been explosive stuff in his hands. His problem, of course, would be how to use it so that it did maximum harm to the boss he didn't like and none at all to himself.

'He was in Charlie Old's bar, and so was I, when my old cricketing chum came in with the news that Matton had been found shot. As it happened I was looking at Donaldson when the old man broke the news and even if I could handle words like the Prof. here I would have a job to tell you exactly what the expression on his face was like. But I can tell you one thing – it wasn't an expression of shock. It wasn't the way a man looks learning something for the first time. I put the memory of that look away into the E.C.B. very carefully. Of course it was natural enough to say if Matton's dead hadn't we better start looking for Roger Tranter; anyone of us might have said it; the fact remains that it was Donaldson who said it first.'

'I wonder what that unpleasant local policeman makes of it all,' Aston said.

Hooky laughed and said in explanation to Dorothea, 'Your friend Herbert included a brush with the local law in his dragon-slaying expedition; the bobby was about to charge a small boy with using a skateboard to the danger of the public and the Prof. rushed in waving a declaration of human rights and civil liberties about.'

'I'm sorry to hear it,' Dorothea said. 'In my opinion skateboards *are* a danger to the public. You ought to be more practical, Herbert.'

'Include me in your disfavour,' Hooky said. 'When the boy in question told me his skateboard was broken I gave him the money to have it repaired.'

'That was compounding a felony,' Dorothea said. 'You should have had more sense.'

'Say rather I was discharging a debt,' Hooky answered. 'Charlie Dent, steeped though he probably is in every sort of juvenile villainy, had done me a service. He told me something which he hadn't told the local policeman. He told me that on Tuesday afternoon, the fatal Tuesday afternoon, he was up in Silverman's Wood birds'-nesting when he ought to have been in school and he saw somebody come out of the old shepherd's hut. And the person he saw was Donaldson.'

A very considerable silence followed this revelation; a silence broken at length by the Professor who said, 'What an extraordinary development.'

'But is it so extraordinary?' Hooky said. 'Not according to my theory, it isn't. Members of the jury, I should say if I were a Q.C. leading for the Crown, you are confronted here with a number of apparently unrelated facts but I venture to think that I can put before you a perfectly plausible theory which will connect and explain them.'

'And what is this famous theory of yours?' Dorothea asked.

'For some reason or other Donaldson, the accountant of Videx, bears Matton, the autocratic head of the firm, a grudge. At Sweeting he learns by chance of the affair between Matton and Mollie, the wife of his chauffeur Roger

Tranter. He is well aware of Roger Tranter's record. If suspicion of the affair got about and harm were to come to Matton, who would almost automatically be suspected? He learns that Tranter is due to go to Reading on company business on Tuesday. He himself arrives in Sweeting in the morning and parks his car in the sunken lane by the church which, especially on a weekday, is very seldom used. He sees the Mercedes come out of Leys' drive and set off for Reading. Tranter won't be back till late afternoon so with hubby safely out of the way it isn't difficult to guess what gypsy-like wife and ardent lover-boy will get up to.

'Only, of course, he means to see that they don't. So mid-morning he shows up at Lodge Cottage.

'Mollie Tranter isn't particularly surprised to see him; he has called there a number of times before with messages from the house. Only this time Donaldson has made up the message himself. Until Mrs Tranter tells us what it was we can only guess at it. It might well have been something about unexpected business having cropped up on the phone so that Matton will be busy all afternoon and will let Roger know later whether he wants the car in the morning or not. Something of that sort. It's easy enough for Mollie Tranter to read between the lines and pick out the bit that affects her. Lover-boy is going to be busy (pounds before poking any day for Matton) so fun and games for the afternoon are off; no point in going up to Silverman's Wood and the love-nest there. So she very sensibly decides to busy herself cleaning out the budgie's cage or doing the ironing, and later going to the shop.

'So far Donaldson's well-thought-out plan is coming along nicely. His next step is to go up to Silverman's Wood and wait. He's pretty certain that, with the husband safely away in Reading and the wife more than willing, Matton will show up. So he waits, the hunter sitting beside the baited trap – though my guess is that he wouldn't sit beside the hut, but in it.

'At Leys Matton has no reason to think that the afternoon assignment is off. It's something he has been looking forward to all morning. Having stoked up his amatory fires with a good lunch he sets out for what he probably describes to Drage as his "constitutional", and I suppose "constitutional" is as good a word for it as any.

'He would be thinking all sorts of pleasant anticipatory thoughts when he ducked his head and went into the hut.

'He is completely knocked off his perch by finding Donaldson there. Donaldson knowing about the Mollie Tranter affair is highly dangerous to him. Whatever the existing quarrel between the two men was it flares up again, intensified. Not that Donaldson cares. That's the way he wants it. He worked out his neat little plan for one purpose and one purpose only; and he puts it into effect. He pulls out his gun and shoots Matton through the head.

'What do you do when you have just shot a man and the acrid tang of the explosion is still in the air? I suppose you look round to make sure you aren't doing anything incredibly stupid like leaving your bowler hat and rolled umbrella behind, something like that. And then you get away out of it just as fast as you can.

'Which, presumably, is what Donaldson did, but with a damned good look round first, when he came out of the hut, to make sure no one was about.

'As far as he could see no one was about; but then one small boy, birds'-nesting when he ought to have been in school, can make himself remarkably hard to see.

' "So far so good," Donaldson thinks and he proceeds to take the next step in his carefully-thought-out plan. He goes down into the village and straight to the front door of Leys.

'When Drage appears in answer to the bell Donaldson says:

' "I think it's just about three-thirty, would you let Sir Frederick know I'm here?"

' "I'm sorry, sir, but Sir Frederick is out."

' "Out? But I've an appointment to see him at half past three."

' "Sir Frederick didn't tell me anything about that, sir."

' "Oh well, I suppose I shall have to wait."

'And wait he did, till it was opening time and he came into the bar of the Arms to tell us what a bore it was when people broke their appointments and kept a man hanging about for hours. And we believed him.'

Hooky finished speaking and there was a thoughtful silence. He pushed his glass forward and said, 'I'll have some more of this excellent Sercial of yours, Herbert, if I may. I haven't done so much talking for years.'

Dorothea filled his glass for him and said, 'And that's your theory, is it?'

'A tenuous thing but mine own,' Hooky averred. 'In the past many a man has been hanged on a less likely story, I can assure you. Some of it is guesswork; but a lot of it can be proved, and will be proved by patient – and when I say patient I should perhaps say merciless – questioning and examination.'

'But what about the chauffeur, Tranter?' the Professor asked.

'Donaldson's big piece of luck. And if you are going round shooting people you need a slice or two of luck, believe me. Roger Tranter gets back from the Reading job earlier than he expected to. He calls in at Lodge Cottage and his wife isn't there. *We* know, now, that she was at the shop, but her husband doesn't know that and it's not her usual afternoon for shopping, so where the hell is she he wonders. One or two things have been half said and hinted at lately which have set him thinking and if that bastard Matton is up to anything there's going to be trouble.

'On an impulse he decides to go up to Silverman's Wood and take a look at the hut up there that he's been hearing odd bits about.

'He doesn't know what he's going to find there; he's ready for anything – except for what in fact he does find – Matton dead with a hole in his head. And that scares the life out of him. He has already been inside once for violence. He's got a record. And once a man has got a record he's marked down by the law. He is automatically suspect number one if there's any trouble around.

'Roger Tranter didn't have to do much thinking; if his wife had been having an affair with the dead man, which he was beginning to suspect, who the hell was going to believe that he hadn't done the killing?

'My guess is that Roger Tranter went straight back to the village, got into the Mercedes; drove as fast as he could to Newhaven and got on the ferry, Mercedes and all; and by this time is somewhere down in the South of France. Which, of course, suits Donaldson's book splendidly.'

'And what are you going to do about it all?' Dorothea asked.

'I'm going to pay one more visit to Sweeting,' Hooky said, 'it's a place I've grown fond of. Especially the Cobalt Arms. I shall seek out that irritating person, but at the same time worthy public servant, P.C. West, and suggest to him that he find out what Charlie Dent can tell him.'

'And you think the boy will talk to him?'

'West may not be one's idea of a bosom chum, but he is very far from being a fool. Once his nose is pointed in the right direction he and his kind will follow the scent to the finish.'

The Professor laid down his pipe, now smoked to its end. 'I must confess,' he said, 'that when I set out with the intention of calling on the head of Videx I had no idea of the unlikely things I should get mixed up in.'

'I think you acquitted yourself extremely well, Herbert,' Dorothea said.

Herbert Aston smiled his acknowledgement of the compliment. 'Well,' he agreed, 'I've had a look at the outside world, at what I suppose some people would have me believe is the world of reality, and, in spite of certain superficial excitements, I can't say that I like it much. I'm glad to be back with you, Dorothea, and with Tennyson's truncated trochaic octometers.'

'And what the hell are they?' Hooky wondered as he took his leave and walked towards Brighton station; but he was

content; if the funny little Prof. and his pet pupil wanted to mull over their truncated trochaic octometers together why should he spoil their fun?

'A hundred and fifty-seven to be precise,' Hooky said. El Vino's in mid-morning: a little too early yet for the flood-tide to be flowing, but not too early for Lewis, a massive figure seated in his accustomed place – had he, indeed, ever left it? Hooky wondered in amused fantasy.

'A hundred and fifty-seven miles,' Lewis said judicially. 'Well, what is it, after all? I expect you feel all the better for having done it. I'd have done it myself when I was a young man and thought nothing of it.'

Hooky laughed; but it was a laugh with reservations. You could never be sure about Lewis. It was quite possible that once the flabby sixteen stones had been a firm twelve, the paunch non-existent, and that he had done prodigious feats for school or university.

'– if ever I *was* a young man,' Lewis continued. 'Sometimes I doubt it. Where did you end up?'

'A place called Sweeting.'

It might have been called the sea-coast of Bohemia as far as Lewis was concerned; in his view anything north of Islington was Arctic waste land and the far side of Hammersmith Bridge the West Country.

'Sweeting?' he said. 'Never heard of it. What goes on there?'

'Oh, you know, the usual things – murder, fornication, seduction.'

'Just suit you,' Lewis said. 'Just your cup of tea. Did you get mixed up in it all?'

'Only as an interested observer.'

'That's all I am now,' Lewis said, 'an interested observer of the farce and, do you know, Hooky, I'm beginning to think it may be a mistake. I think the Japanese have got it just about right, do you remember what they say?'

Hooky had to admit that lately he had fallen behind slightly in his Japanese reading.

'Those who dance are fools, those who look on are fools; so we may as well dance.'

Hooky pushed his glass forward; he watched while Lewis tilted the bottle and filled the glass, his thoughts running on sweet sherry and the woman who liked it; on Dorothea; on the Professor who had played Don Quixote; on the woodland hut and a dead man lying inside it – a queer, multi-coloured tapestry, he thought, who knows who weaves it and why and where it's all going to end . . .

He raised his glass. Outside Fleet Street was noisy with traffic. People were beginning to come in. Talk, the everlasting usual talk, was beginning to flow.

'Here's to honest rogues and bastards,' Hooky said, 'and on with the dance.'